**BEWARE!
DO NOT READ THIS
BOOK FROM BEGINNING TO END!**

You and your family are visiting an exhibit from ancient Egypt when you make a discovery of your own: a 4000-year-old diary written by a mummy! Cool, you think, as you slip the book into your pocket.

But then you find out the mummy is alive! And he wants more than just his diary back . . .

He wants your BODY! And you've got to find a way to stop him!

There are clues in the diary to help you. But first you'll have to decode ancient hieroglyphic writing. Or journey to the pyramids in Egypt.

Can you unlock the secrets of the mad mummy's diary before he gets you under wraps?

This scary adventure is all about you. You decide what will happen. And you decide how terrifying the scares will be.

Start on page 1. Then follow the instructions at the bottom of each page. You make the choices.

If you make the right choices, you will escape the revenge of the mad mummy. You may even find his burial chamber filled with golden treasures! If you make the wrong choice . . . BEWARE!

SO TAKE A LONG, DEEP BREATH, CROSS YOUR FINGERS AND TURN TO PAGE 1 NOW TO *GIVE YOURSELF GOOSEBUMPS!*

READER BEWARE—
YOU CHOOSE THE SCARE!

Look for more
GIVE YOURSELF GOOSEBUMPS adventures
from R.L. STINE:

Give Yourself Goosebumps

Diary of a Mad Mummy

R.L. Stine

Hippo

Scholastic Children's Books
Commonwealth House, 1–19 New Oxford Street, London WC1A 1NU, UK
a division of Scholastic Ltd
London ~ New York ~ Toronto ~ Sydney ~ Auckland

First published in the USA by Scholastic Inc., 1996
First published in the UK by Scholastic Ltd, 1998

ISBN 0 590 11335 6

Typeset by Rowland Phototypesetting Ltd, Bury St Edmunds, Suffolk
Printed by Cox & Wyman Ltd, Reading, Berks.

10 9 8 7 6 5 4 3 2 1

"Welcome to San Francisco," the tour guide says. Her voice echoes in the marble lobby of the office building. "This is the famous Pyramid Building—the city's most famous skyscraper."

"When do we get to see the mummy?" your five-year-old sister whines at your side.

You cringe and squeeze Susie's hand. You wish you didn't have to drag her around. But taking care of her is always your job on family holidays.

Oh, well, you think. Who cares? This is going to be the best holiday ever. You and your family are staying in a hotel in downtown San Francisco. You have a view of the whole city from your window—including the tall, spindly Pyramid Building just a few blocks away. And this month, there's a display of ancient Egyptian artifacts in the lobby. Including a real mummy! You can't wait to see it!

"I want the mummy!" Susie whines again.

"I want my mummy! I want my mummy!" your older brother Derek chants, imitating Susie's babyish voice.

You laugh at Derek's joke. Then you whisper to Susie, "We'll see it as soon as that tour group gets out of the way."

You peer through the crowd at the mummy in his glass case.

Hey! Did the mummy just move?

Turn to PAGE 2.

2

Your heart starts pounding. It can't be! But you know you just saw the mummy's arm move!

Didn't anyone else see it?

You stare hard at the brightly lit display cases in the middle of the lobby. A tour group crowds around the glass, blocking your view. So you stand on your tiptoes. Under a pinkish halogen light, you can see an ancient bandaged mummy lying in a beautiful, gold-painted wooden box.

It's the first mummy you've ever seen. A king from more than four thousand years ago.

A dead person.

Something about it gives you the creeps.

The tour group moves away, and the lobby clears. "Come on!" Susie squeals, pulling you towards the mummy's case. A strange chill runs up your spine as you step closer.

You gaze at the mummy's face and shudder. It is hideous. Part of his face is still wrapped up—but part of it isn't. You can see his dried, leathery skin stretched tightly over his shrunken, bony nose.

You back away—and your foot bumps into something on the floor.

Turn to PAGE 3.

You glance down to see what you've kicked.

"Hey—look!" you cry out softly.

But no one is listening. The tour group has scattered. Susie has let go of your hand. She's pressing her nose to the glass in front of the wooden mummy case. As usual, your fourteen-year-old brother, Derek, is acting as if he doesn't know any of you. He's talking to some kids by the door. Your parents are examining another display case.

No one notices what you've found on the floor. You pick it up. It's a small clump of folded pages tied together at the edge with dried grass. It looks like some kind of ancient book.

You open it carefully. The pages seem as if they might crumble in your hands. You peer at the squiggly markings on the page. To your surprise you recognize words . . . they're in English! The handwriting is hard to read, but finally you work out what it says:

"This is the first day in my tomb. I am wrapped so tightly that I fear I may never breathe again. The bandages that preserve me are a prison. I am a king, yet they have brought me here, drained me of my blood, and bound me with bandages. Against my will! Stop! I beg them. Do not do this horrible thing! I am not dead! I am alive!"

Keep reading on PAGE 4.

Your mouth drops open as you flip through the ancient pages. Could this be a diary of some kind? A *mummy's* diary? Written four thousand years ago!

But why isn't it in ancient hieroglyphics? How can it be in English?

This is weird. Definitely weird. But somehow, in your heart, you know the diary is real. Every word of it is true.

You glance round again. No one notices you. You turn to another page and read on.

"I am embalmed alive. Me. The pharaoh. The king! And why? For one reason only. Because, upon my neck, I bear a strange birthmark—a red stain in a strange shape that frightens my people. They think it is a sign of evil.

"Even I am not sure what it means. Does it really mean I am evil? Could I actually hurt people? Am I mad?"

Your hands tremble as you flip to another page and read on.

"Each night my spirit walks the earth. For centuries. Each night my spirit writes this diary. But now, at last, my chance has come. Tonight, my body will walk the earth! Tonight, here in this strangest of all pyramids, I will escape my prison!"

Turn to PAGE 9.

The American looks like a nice guy. You think he's someone you can trust. And he might be able to help you get home. You decide to show him the diary.

"Hmmm," the American says, taking a magnifying glass from his suit pocket. He flips through the pages, studying them. "Verrrry interesting."

"Don't trust him!" the Egyptian guard whispers in your ear. "He's a thief!"

"I heard that. And I certainly am not a thief," the American declares. "My name is Webster MacArthur Woobly the third. But just call me Web. I'm a professor of ancient studies at Cairo University. And you are . . . ?"

You introduce yourself.

"Nice to meet you," Web Woobly says. "Can I buy you a glass of lemonade in town? Cairo is just a few miles from here, and I'd like to talk to you about obtaining this diary."

Obtaining? As in buying it? Hmmm—sounds good to you!

"Don't go with him!" the Egyptian warns you.

Last chance to change your mind . . .

If you still trust Web Woobly, turn to PAGE 28.

If you trust the Egyptian instead, turn to PAGE 22.

Let the mummy take Susie? You can't do it.

"No way," you tell the mummy, your voice shaking. "Take me—but leave her alone."

"Yes . . ." the mummy whispers in his hoarse, raspy voice. He grips your wrist with his gauzy bandaged hand and starts to drag you out of the hotel.

"Wait," you tell the mummy. "I need to get my jacket." The mummy stares at you a moment, then releases you.

"Don't worry," you whisper to Derek as you grab your jacket. "I'm just going with him so he won't hurt Susie. But I'll get away from him as soon as we're outside."

"Okay," Derek whispers back. "I'll follow you."

"No . . . you . . . won't," the mummy says to Derek. Then he points a bandaged finger at Derek's head. Instantly, your brother is frozen stiff. He can't move!

But you can, so move over to PAGE 53.

Nobody seems to be around. Nothing but sand. Egypt's hot sun beats down on you, making you feel dizzy and faint. You'd like to sit down in the shade, but there isn't any.

Water, you think. I must have water . . .

Now you know why they say things like that in old films. You've never been so thirsty in your life.

Luckily, you had a light jacket with you in San Francisco. It's tied round your waist. You take it off and hold it over your head, using it as a tent for shade.

You open the diary to the first page with writing. It's page seven. You study the hieroglyphs. They look like this:

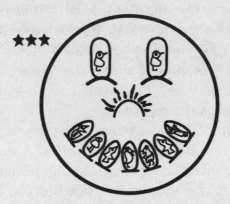

What do you think it means? If it looks like a bunch of birds sitting around a camp-fire to you, turn to PAGE 58.

If you see an ancient Egyptian smiley face instead, turn to PAGE 12.

"No!" you cry out. You stare into the wooden box.

The mummy has gone! And something else is in its place.

Gold! Tons of it. Coins, little statues, sceptres and crowns. All made of gold.

For a moment, you can't believe it. Is this some kind of illusion? Is there a trapdoor in the box? A sliding panel? Or mirrors? You've seen this kind of thing done by magicians on TV.

You lean into the box and feel the bottom and sides with both hands.

It's solid.

You pick up one of the coins and bite it.

It's really gold.

I suppose the chant worked! you say to yourself. Maybe the mummy has come back to life in Egypt. Maybe he went back to his own time and sent this gold to thank me. He said he was a king, didn't he? Then you hear a sound that makes you turn round.

"Thank . . . you," a voice whispers, echoing in the empty lobby. It's the familiar voice of the mummy, with the wheezing sound between each word. But the mummy is nowhere to be seen. "Thank . . . you . . . for . . . saving . . . my . . . life," he says. "I . . . hope . . . this . . . gold . . . can . . . repay . . . you . . . in . . . some . . . small . . . way . . . And . . . now . . . I, . . . King . . . Buthramaman, . . . bid . . . you . . . farewell."

THE END

Can it be possible?

Is the mummy going to escape *tonight*? How?

And is *this* the "strangest of all pyramids"? The Pyramid Building? It would seem strange to some old pharaoh, you suppose.

You read over the same pages again—trying to make sense of them.

"Each night my spirit writes this diary," it says.

No way! you think. He isn't writing with his hand. He's writing with his mind! The mummy *thinks* something, and it appears on the page.

Amazing.

You shoot a quick, sideways glance to make sure the lobby guard isn't watching. Then you tuck the diary under your shirt.

Turn to PAGE 132.

Frantically, you glance round for somewhere to hide. Anywhere.

You spot a storage cupboard close by. The door stands slightly open. Yes! you think, as you quickly slip inside.

You flip on a light, hold your breath and listen. Are the footsteps coming towards you?

You wait. Your heart pounds.

Finally the footsteps pass.

You breathe and glance round at the supplies in the cupboard.

Rolls of toilet paper. Soaps. Tiny bottles of hotel shampoo. Towels. Mops. A vacuum cleaner.

And pens! Ballpoint pens with the hotel's name on them. Small note pads, too. There are some just like them by the telephone in your room.

That's what you need, you realize. Paper and pen, so you can write your family a note!

You start to scribble a note to your brother, Derek.

But suddenly you notice something else on the cupboard floor. Something even better than a pen. Keys! The housekeeper could have dropped them, you decide. They look like master keys that will open every room in the hotel.

If you use the keys to open your hotel room, turn to PAGE 41.

If you write a note and slip it to Derek, turn to PAGE 117.

"Younger," you repeat. "Okay. We can do that."

Quickly, you hop out of the sarcophagus so he can't close you in. "Follow me," you tell him.

Snaking your way through the streets of San Francisco, you lead the mummy to a building a few blocks away. It's a glass-and-chrome-fronted building with a fancy sign painted on the door.

THE HEAVEN-ON-EARTH HEALTH SPA.

You remember this place because you've passed it every day on the way to your hotel. And it's open twenty-four hours a day!

"What's ... this?" the mummy asks. He stands back from the door, hesitant to go in. In fact, he's acting a little shy.

"It's a health spa," you explain. "A fancy place where they give you health drinks, mud baths and things like that. They make you look younger. That's their job."

"Really?" the mummy whispers.

Although it seems impossible, you almost see a flicker of a smile spread across his lips.

You lead the way into the spa and approach the receptionist.

"Uh, hi," you stammer. "My, uh, friend, here, wants to get a skin treatment."

The receptionist eyes the mummy suspiciously. "Does he have an appointment?" she asks.

An appointment? Uh-oh. Think fast on PAGE 99.

12

"Looks like an ancient Egyptian smiley face to me," you say out loud.

Uh-oh. You're talking to yourself. And you're seeing smiley faces. You'd better find some water soon!

You suddenly remember that you had a packet of Fruity Bites sweets in your pocket. You reach for them. They're still there! And they've only melted a little.

You pop two in your mouth. Ahhhhhhh.

They almost make you forget your parched throat.

Almost.

But not for long.

Get up and search for water on PAGE 24.

The three men lean closer and peer into your sarcophagus.

"Yeow-sa!" the other guard yells. "He's starting to rot!"

No! you think. But it's true! Your ancient, mummified body is turning to mush! Your face is losing its shape. Your hollow, ancient eyes are caving in, leaving huge holes in your face.

No wonder you feel so weak!

"It's the salt air!" the man with the deep voice cries. His eyes open in horror as pieces of your body begin to fall away!

"Without bandages to protect it from the fog and salty air, the dried flesh is mouldering and breaking down."

"What should we do with him?" George asks, holding his nose.

"He's no good to us now," the man with the deep voice answers. "We've got to get rid of him."

"No," the other guard insists. "I say we take him back to the museum."

"Toss a coin," George declares. "That's how we'll decide."

Oh, no, you think. Not another coin!

Toss another coin. If it's heads, turn to PAGE 35.

If it's tails, turn to PAGE 27.

14

See what's inside? Are they kidding?

The doctors close in on you, rubbing their hands together eagerly. "I'm going to enjoy this," Stuart says with a creepy smile.

"Let's find out what's in there," Dr Lacey adds eagerly.

You stare at the surgical tools in terror. You want to scream. You want to yell for help. But when you open your mouth, no sound comes out.

You can't talk!

You'll never be able to explain that you're really a kid! What will you do?

You're desperate to escape. You scan the room, searching for something—anything— that will help you. You spot a chemical beaker full of some kind of clear liquid. You pick up the beaker and throw the liquid in Dr Lacey's face!

"Hey!" she sputters. "He just threw water at me!"

Water? Your heart sinks. That was the only plan you had. And it didn't work.

These doctors are definitely going to open you up!

Turn to PAGE 31.

You enter the cool, dark tomb with Mohammed right behind you. He carries a torch to light the way.

The passageway, a narrow corridor made of large stone blocks, is creepy. You feel as if someone—or something—might jump out at you at any minute.

You walk a few more steps forward and come to a place where the passageway splits into a fork, or a Y.

"Which way?" you ask.

"Follow your heart," Mohammed answers mysteriously.

My heart? you think. Is that some kind of clue?

Let's see.

Your heart is on the left. Is that what he means? Should you take the passage to the left?

You peer down the left passageway and see nothing but darkness. A horrible, empty darkness—as if no one has ever returned from that path.

Then you peer down the passageway to the right. It looks wider than the other one and brighter. It isn't nearly as dark.

If you take the passageway to the left, turn to PAGE 123.

If you take the passageway to the right, turn to PAGE 79.

16

Your bandages, the ones the mummy-kid is unwrapping, have trailed across his arms.

All at once, they start to wrap themselves round him just as they had mysteriously clung to you. They bind him quickly. Tightly. They seem to have a life of their own, as if they want to choke him to death.

The mummy-kid's eyes flash with fear.

"No!" he cries, trying to pull away.

Yes! you think. This is it! This is how I can swap places with him again!

If you can just get all the bandages off in time . . .

Then they'll wrap round him, just as they wrapped round you in the lobby of the Pyramid Building.

As fast as you can, you start to unwrap the rest of your bandages.

Quickly you unwrap the horrible gauze so that it will be free to encircle the mummy. The bandages wind themselves round his face, his neck, his body. They pin his arms to his sides so he can't move!

Turn to PAGE 111.

The guard tosses a coin and it comes up tails.

"Good," George says. "I win. Now listen to me."

You listen, too, from inside your mummy case in the boot.

But you can't hear a thing. And a moment later, George slams the boot shut and the car takes off.

Whoa! you want to cry as you feel the car zooming up and down the famous San Francisco hills. Your stomach would be turning over right now—if you had one—the hills are so steep. It feels as if you're on a roller-coaster.

George drives like a maniac. You can hear the tyres squeal round the corners as he makes sharp turns.

Finally the car slows down and eases to a stop.

Where are we? you wonder.

You hear a foghorn. And the sound of water lapping at the sides of a pier. You figure you must be near a dock. You can almost smell the salty air from inside the wooden case.

Why would they bring me to a pier? you wonder. Then you get a sinking feeling.

Turn to PAGE 55.

18

The guard could be making the noise. Or it could be the mummy.

Either way, you won't want to be found.

Hide—fast!

You dash across the lobby and dart behind a pillar.

SCRAPE . . . SCRAPE . . .

It sounds as if someone is dragging his feet across the floor. And whoever it is, is still coming your way.

Who could it be?

You are halfway to the exit. Your knees tremble with fear, but you can't help being curious.

You have to make a decision.

If you stay to find out who it is, turn to PAGE 45.

If you leave now and go back to the hotel, turn to PAGE 88.

Before you can protest, Web Woobly climbs on to another camel. As soon as his camel starts walking, yours follows.

"Where are we going?" you ask nervously. Suddenly, this doesn't seem like a great idea. Especially since the camel isn't very comfortable to sit on. And boy, does it stink!

"To Cairo," Web replies.

Slowly the two of you make the bumpy nine-mile camel ride to the capital city of Egypt, When you arrive, Web takes you to a small cafe on a busy street and orders you the promised glass of lemonade.

"Now, my young friend," Web says. "Let's talk about the diary. How does two thousand dollars sound?"

Well—how *does* it sound?

If you like Web's offer, take it on PAGE 63.

If you think you can get more, bargain with him on PAGE 114.

20

A dead mummy coming alive again? You want to see that!

You hold the diary hidden inside your shirt and look around for Susie. "Coming, Mother!" you say. You'll come back tonight and find out if what the diary says is really true.

"See you later," you whisper to the mummy. He looks completely dead to you. But ... you know you saw his arm move.

You keep the diary hidden in your shirt during dinner in Chinatown. You never get a chance to read it. Back at the hotel, Susie is hungry again. She insists on ordering from room service, but they never show up. She wants to stay up waiting, but eventually your parents make you all go to bed.

Finally, when everyone else is asleep, you sneak out of the hotel. The cool, foggy night air makes you shiver as you walk two blocks to the Pyramid Building. The streets are empty at this time of night.

When you reach the building, you slip in through the open front door—and find the lobby guard asleep. He's sitting on a stool, slumped over a tall reception desk. A small light on his desk gives the cavernous lobby an eerie glow.

You step past the guard, towards the displays in the centre of the lobby. After a minute, your eyes adjust to the dim light.

Then you spot it—and gasp!

The glass case holding the mummy is broken. The mummy has gone!

Turn to PAGE 36.

Get into a sarcophagus? No possible way, you decide.

With a desperate pull, you yank your arm away from the mummy.

Ooooh . . . bad idea.

Remember how the mummy had your wrist in an iron grip, like a vice? Remember how strong he was?

Well . . . close your eyes.

What happens next is too horrible to go into. You really don't want the gory details.

Let's just say that your arm—the one the mummy was holding?—well, he's still holding it.

And you aren't.

Which means that even if there were another page to turn to right now, you wouldn't be able to turn to it. Not while still holding this book with your one remaining hand!

Face it. You've come up short-handed in this story.

THE END

You decide to trust the young Egyptian guard. He seems genuinely concerned. You hand him the diary.

The American looks disappointed, but he turns and wanders away.

The Egyptian man tells you his name is Mohammed. Then he examines the diary, his eyes widening. "This diary must be returned to the royal tomb of Buthramaman," he cries. "Only then will the mummy rest. Come with me!"

"But where are we going?" you ask him.

"To the tomb," he whispers. His eyes narrow and his eyebrows curl in, making him look as if he has a deep, dark secret.

Mohammed leads you by donkey to the Nile River. There, you board a boat and travel south all day and all night. Finally you reach a strange, uninhabited part of Egypt. In the steamy heat, he leads you through a lush jungle, and then to another desert area, and finally to the sandy, stone entrance to the tomb.

"You go in first," he says, pointing the way.

Me? you think. Why me?

Turn to PAGE 73.

You slam the door shut. "It's him!" you whisper to Derek. "It's got to be!" You lean all your weight against the door. No way is the mummy getting in!

KNOCK. KNOCK-KNOCK.

"It can't be the mummy, dummy," Derek says, hopping off his camp-bed. He stomps over to the door and shoves you aside. "I mean, is a mummy going to *knock* politely on the door?"

KNOCK. KNOCK.

"Don't open it!" you beg. You reach for the doorknob to try to stop him.

Too late. Derek swings open the door.

Standing there in the dimly lit hallway is a small figure wrapped in ancient bandages.

The mummy!

Before you or Derek can stop him, the mummy pushes through the doorway. There's a mummy standing in your hotel room! You can hardly believe it.

"You . . . stole . . . my . . . life . . ." the mummy whispers slowly. "Now . . . I . . . will . . . take . . . my . . . revenge."

You are too stunned to move. All you can do is turn to PAGE 38.

If you don't find water soon, you know you'll definitely be a goner. So you stagger forward, sucking on the Fruity Bites. Then you see it!

Another smiley face!

Maybe you really are going mad.

It's on that sand dune not far from you. A row of Egyptian statues. Bird-faced pillars carved in stone, like ones you've seen in books on ancient Egypt.

Two statues make the eyes and seven more make the mouth. Exactly like the drawing in the diary! You pull out the diary. Turn to PAGE 7 and check it again.

The face in the diary has a nose. There's no nose with the statues. But you figure that could just be a picture of the sun. To show how HOT it is in the desert. That would make sense.

What doesn't make sense is why the ancient Egyptians put a smiley face design in the middle of the desert! And why the mummy's diary has a picture of it!

Run over to the statues on PAGE 133 and get some answers!

For an instant, you consider not completing the spell. But you can't. Not after you've given your word.

And besides, the mummy seems so lonely.

"*Teki Kahru Teki Kahra Teki Khari!*" you chant quickly, before you lose your nerve again.

You hold your breath, waiting for the mummy to come back to life.

Silence. Nothing happens.

The lobby of the Pyramid Building is even quieter than before. A strange stillness hangs in the air. It's as if the whole world has suddenly come to a grinding halt.

A horrible thought creeps into your head. Is everyone *dead*?

You glance over at the guard. He looks like he's asleep, but he's not snoring any more. If he's asleep, it's a deep, dreamless sleep.

Sweat trickles down your neck while you wait for the mummy case to open.

Nothing. Nothing but silence and the sound of your own heartbeat.

Finally you can't stand it any longer. You reach over and open the lid.

What will you find inside? Turn to PAGE 8.

The hallway turns a few more times. But there aren't any more choices. No more forks.

Finally you see a glimmer of light.

Light? Where's it coming from?

You turn the corner and spot the answer.

The lift!

At last—you're in the basement of the Pyramid Building!

Aren't you?

You run to the lift and push the UP button over and over. You hope that if you press it harder, it'll come faster.

Yeah. Sure. As if that's ever worked.

Press it again on PAGE 56.

They toss a coin. "Tails," George declares.

Uh-oh. Big trouble. Major bummer.

"Toss him overboard," the man with the deep voice orders. "And get it over with!"

Those are the last words you ever hear.

A second later, George and the other guard fling you over the side of the boat. The chilly water soaks into you. You start to sink.

You never could swim, even as a kid.

But what's not the worst part.

The worst part is that these coastal waters are shark-infested.

And as it turns out, mummies make great fish food!

THE END

You decide to trust Web Woobly.

He seems friendly. And with a name like that, how bad could he be? Besides, you like the sound of his offer. Lemonade—and possibly big money for the diary!

You'll worry about getting home later. Your new American pal may be able to help you.

"A cool drink would be very refreshing," Web Woobly says, wiping the sweat from his forehead. "Let's go."

He puts one hand up in the air, as if he's hailing a taxi in New York City. Then he sticks two fingers in his mouth and whistles.

Almost at once, a man on a camel rides up.

"Need a lift, buddy?" the camel driver asks.

"Yes," Web Woobly says. Then he speaks a few words in Arabic to the camel driver. Pretty soon, the camel kneels down.

"Climb up," Web instructs you.

You do. But as soon as you're seated on the camel, you start to feel guilty. You *know* you're not supposed to get in cars with strangers! Is getting on a camel so different?

"Uh, I think I'll get down," you start to say.

"Too late," Web Woobly announces with a small laugh.

Turn to PAGE 19.

You have to hide! You duck into the alcove of a nearby building and huddle in the shadows. The long, black limousine cruises by.

Phew. Close one.

Except an instant later the two glass doors behind you swing open and two doctors walk out. One man, one woman.

That's when you notice the sign over the entrance: EMERGENCY MEDICAL ASSISTANCE.

"Hey," the male doctor says to you. "What are you doing out here? You should be in bed. You are *very* ill!"

Then the female doctor steps closer. She peers into your face. At your shrunken, dried, brown-leather face.

She grabs your wrist.

"Hey, look!" she whispers to the other doctor. "This isn't a patient. It's a mummy!"

Turn to PAGE 86.

Before you can jump away, the mummy's hand darts out and he grabs your wrist. He picks up the tail end of one of his bandages, a long one that has come partly unwrapped. Quickly, he uses it to tie your wrists behind your back—like a prisoner! Then he does the same thing to Derek!

For an old dead man, he moves really fast!

The instant the bandage touches you, you feel your skin begin to wither and harden and shrivel. Your arms and legs grow stiff—so stiff you can barely move.

He yanks the bandages, and you and Derek both stumble towards the mummy. He wraps more of the ancient strips round and round your bodies.

"What's happening?" you start to ask Derek.

But when you glance at Derek's face, you let out a horrible scream.

Derek's face is brown and leather-hard—just like the mummy's! And what's more, his eyes have gone!

Only two deep, empty eye sockets remain! You stare into them, deeper and deeper, feeling yourself getting dizzy. It almost makes you pass out in disgust.

Hurry to PAGE 76!

"Hold him down," Stuart yells. "I'll set up the X-ray machine."

X-rays? Is that all they're going to do?

Oh.

That won't be so bad. Maybe it will even be interesting.

You stop struggling and cooperate as the two doctors X-ray each and every part of your body. Even your head!

A short while later, Stuart strolls out of the darkroom, holding the X-rays up to the light.

"I don't believe it," he mutters.

"What did you find?" Dr Lacey asks Stuart. She stands next to him and peers at the X-rays.

"He has no organs. No heart. No stomach. No brain," Stuart answers. "Of course, I didn't expect him to since he's a mummy."

"Then what's so unusual?" Dr Lacey demands.

"This," Stuart says. "Look what I found inside his head!"

Dr Lacey takes an X-ray from Stuart and holds it up to the light. She gasps.

"Astonishing!" Dr Lacey exclaims. "Amazing!"

"Extraordinary!" Stuart adds.

What's going on? Aren't they going to tell *you*? After all, it's your head!

Find out what's in there on PAGE 125.

"Yes," you tell the mummy. "I know a secret chant that will bring you back to life."

"What . . . is . . . it?" the mummy asks, wheezing between each word. He sounds eager.

"*Klatu Barrada Nicto*," you recite. You close your eyes and say it again, like a chant. "*Klatu Barrada Nicto*."

"Ha!" the mummy exclaims, almost laughing. "*Klatu . . . Barrada . . . Nicto?* That . . . is . . . from . . . an . . . old . . . film! You . . . know . . . *nothing*. You . . . are . . . doomed!"

Uh-oh. He's right. Those are the words the alien speaks in the old 1950s sci-fi film, *The Day the Earth Stood Still*.

You're in big trouble now.

Turn to PAGE 48.

George holds you down while the other guard closes the sarcophagus lid. Tight.

Help! you want to scream as the darkness closes in on you.

Then you're thrown against the side of the sarcophagus.

The guards have lifted you up on to their shoulders and are carrying you somewhere!

At first you bang on the sarcophagus lid with both fists. *Let me out!* you silently scream.

Then you lie very still and listen.

From the guards' muffled conversation, you work out what's happening. They are carrying the wooden mummy case to a car and loading it into the boot.

"Now what?" George asks the other guard.

"Now we take him back to the museum," the other man replies.

"No way!" you hear George exclaim. "Are you kidding? We've got a living mummy here! We could make a fortune!"

From inside the sarcophagus, you hear the other man mumble something. George answers back. It sounds like they're arguing. You hear George exclaim, "Okay, we'll toss a coin for it! Heads, you win. Tails, we do what I say."

Uh-oh. Your life depends on the toss of a coin!

Toss a coin. If it comes up heads, turn to PAGE 67.

If it's tails, turn to PAGE 17.

34

Derek is laughing uncontrollably. "I got you!" he squeals, pointing at you. "I really got you!"

"Got me?" you stammer. "What do you mean, got me?"

"The mummy! The diary!" He wipes the tears of laughter away from his eyes. "I made the whole thing up.

"I brought this diary from home," Derek explains. "I made this paper in art class. I knew we were going to see the mummy when we got to San Francisco. So I thought up the diary scam. Then I dropped this in the lobby of the Pyramid Building, by your feet. I knew you'd fall for it. You'll believe anything!"

"Mum!" you complain, and try to kick Derek in the shins.

But your mum fails to see you as the victim that you are. After she's helped the waiter up and handed him some money, she sends both of you to bed—for a whole day!

And since you and Derek share the same hotel room, you can't escape his teasing.

Then something occurs to you. What about the mummy? He *did* escape last night. You were there. You saw the broken glass.

Turn to PAGE 96.

The man with the deep voice tosses a coin. It's heads.

"Okay, take him back to the museum," the man agrees. "But do it now. We sail in two minutes. Get him off my ship!"

Clumsily, the two guards throw the lid back on the sarcophagus and haul you off the ship. An hour later, you arrive at the San Francisco Fine Arts Museum. They hand you over to Marvin DeNeely, the museum director who's in charge of Egyptian collections.

"What have you done to him?" Marvin shouts when he glances in the wooden sarcophagus. "My beautiful mummy! He's a mess!"

I'm not really a mummy! you want to cry. I'm a kid!

But with your body rotting away, you can't even manage to sit up. Pieces of your old, hard flesh fall off in chunks. It makes you weak. And dizzy.

You lie in your sarcophagus. Too tired even to cry.

Turn to PAGE 101.

36

You stare at the display case. Your hands are clammy. Your heart beats faster.

You can't believe it. Has the mummy really escaped?

All the other glass cases are fine. There's a fancy golden throne in one, a large, feather-shaped fan in another. Only the mummy display case is broken. Only the mummy has gone.

You've missed it. You're too late.

Broken glass litters the floor at your feet. It seems as if the mummy practically exploded out of his case!

Slowly, you inch closer. You glance down, avoiding the glass. That's when you spot it. A trail of old cloth bandages. Not just one, either. A whole bunch of them.

You know this is crazy, but it looks as if the mummy unwrapped himself as he ran away!

You can't see the bandages very well in the dark. So you bend over to pick one up. But something stops you.

A noise.

Someone is coming from the far side of the lobby. You'd better get out of there—fast!

If you pick up the bandage, turn to PAGE 51.
If you think you'd better run, turn to PAGE 18.

"I know a secret chant," you tell the mummy. "If I say it five times, it will bring you back to life."

You start to chant the powerful magic words. *"Teki Kahru Teki Kahra Te—"*

"Wait!" the mummy cries, holding up his hand. "I . . . know . . . that . . . chant! It . . . *does* . . . work. But . . . I . . . am . . . not . . . ready . . . yet."

The mummy holds out his bandaged hands to help you out of the sarcophagus. Then he quickly takes your place in the box. He seems almost to smile as he settles back into the mummy case.

"All . . . right," the mummy says. "Close . . . the . . . lid . . . and . . . say . . . the . . . words."

"I don't get it," you say. "Why do you want to come back to life in the mummy case?"

The mummy gives you a sad, far-away gaze before answering. "That . . . is . . . the . . . only . . . way," he tells you. "My . . . diary . . . would . . . have . . . brought . . . me . . . to . . . life . . . now—in . . . this . . . wonderful . . . time . . . of . . . yours. But . . . your . . . magic . . . is . . . different. It . . . works . . . another . . . way."

"Another way? How?" you ask.

"Never . . . mind," the mummy warns you. Then he nearly shouts. "Just . . . say . . . the . . . words. *Now!*"

Turn to PAGE 84.

The mummy's hands shoot out and grab your throat! He pulls you towards him.

"Revenge . . . will . . . be . . . mine . . ." The soft wheezing sound between each word the mummy speaks is terrible. It fills your ears, making you shudder.

You struggle against his grip. His hands tighten on your neck. You can hardly breathe.

Why isn't Derek helping you? You glance at him. Derek's standing next to you, wide-eyed, mouth hanging open, frozen with fear.

"Derek!" you try to say. Only it comes out as "D-acckk" because the mummy's grip is so tight on your throat.

Finally Derek snaps out of it. He lunges towards the mummy. But the mummy backs away, still grasping you by the throat.

The mummy lets out a wheezing breath. "Give . . . me . . . the . . . diary—or else!"

Turn to PAGE 105.

Your life is in danger! Why?

The wild, worried look in the Arab man's eyes tells you not to ask questions. You don't have time! He presses the camel's lead-rope into your hands and repeats his warning.

"Go!"

Go where? you wonder as you mount the camel. And why me?

You ride out of town as fast as you can.

The further away from the Mouski you get, the better you feel.

Except . . .

Is someone following you?

Suddenly, you're almost positive there's someone on your tail.

Try a sneaky manoeuvre to get away. Turn to PAGE 56, then 92, then 103, then 24, then back to 56 again. Don't read those pages, silly! Just turn to them. Maybe that will confuse whoever is following you. Then sneak over to PAGE 52 and see if you've lost them.

You decide to open the door.

But your heart is racing. What if it *is* the mummy and he knows you took his diary? Will he be angry?

In one swift, action-packed move, you fling open the door, take a flying leap, and karate-kick the person standing there.

KA-POW! He tumbles halfway across the hallway.

Uh-oh. Big mistake.

Turn to PAGE 57.

Forget writing a note, you decide. You want to see your family again. You want to confront that creep—that mummy—who has stolen your life!

You pick up the keys and flip through them. You spot one with a small piece of masking tape on it. In blue ink, someone has written the word MASTER on the tape.

That's it! The key that will open your family's door!

You race down the hall. The key fits. Just as you had hoped. In an instant, you turn the lock and burst into your family's hotel room.

To your surprise, they're all sitting there wide awake . . . waiting for you.

Including the mummy. Who looks exactly like you used to!

"Aaaahhhh!" Susie screams when she sees you. "Aaaahhhh! Get him away!"

"I told you!" the mummy who looks like you shouts. "I told you he was following me!"

"Grab him, Derek! Quick!" your dad says.

Turn to PAGE 92.

The mummy, who looks exactly like you, moves forward into the storage cupboard. He pushes you back, forcing you against the cupboard wall. You're trapped!

"I got your note," he grumbles. He reaches into his pyjama pocket—your pyjamas!—and pulls out the crumpled paper you wrote on. He throws it in your face. "Forget it! You're never going to get your body back! I've been waiting too long for this chance—my chance to have a life!"

Still pinning you against the back cupboard wall with one hand, he grabs at your bandages with the other. The bandages that wrapped themselves round you all by themselves. You try to fight him off, but he's stronger. He unwraps you from the top, unwinding the bandages that encircle your head.

"You won't last long without these," he says. "Your body will soon start to rot and then—ahh!"

All at once, he jumps back. A look of terror flashes into his eyes.

Turn to PAGE 16.

43

You decide to duck into the lift.

With the diary tucked under your shirt, you casually stroll over and push the UP button. But the first lift that arrives is going down.

Oh, well. That'll do.

Quickly, you slip into the lift. Luckily no one else gets in with you. Your parents don't even notice you've gone.

Great, you think as the car whooshes downwards. Now you can read the diary in private.

DING. A bell rings as the doors open to the basement.

"Weird," you say as you step out of the lift.

This is the *basement*?

To your amazement, the place looks as if it were built thousands of years ago. The walls are made of huge blocks of rough, tan stone. The only light shines from a fixture over the lift doors. In the dim glow, you can see that the lifts are the only modern-looking part of the basement.

Cautiously, you walk down a strange, dark hallway. Your trainers scrape against the stones.

It's really too dark to read the diary. But you can't help wanting to explore.

The diary can wait, you decide.

Explore the basement on PAGE 49.

"Here. Take it!" You thrust the diary into the mummy's bandaged hands.

HSSSSSSSSSS . . .

The mummy lets out a long, raspy sound like a sigh. You could swear his expression has changed. His face seems to soften with relief.

"Ahhh, yesss . . ." the mummy says, clasping the diary to his chest. "Now . . . all . . . I . . . need . . . is . . ."

Another long wheeze escapes from his mouth before he speaks the last word.

"You!"

Turn to PAGE 30.

You decide to stay hidden behind the pillar. You want to find out if it's the mummy. You have to see if the mummy has really come back to life!

SCRAPE ... SCRAPE ...

The footsteps sound nearer ... nearer ...

You can't stand it any more! You peek your head round the corner.

The figure steps into the dim light of the lobby from a nearby hall.

It's the mummy!

And he's alive!

Turn to PAGE 62.

There's a big, ugly crocodile on the steps in front of you. Crocodiles mean water. That means there must be some near by! But right about now, crocodiles mostly mean danger.

It's as if he's guarding the gold.

You freeze. Don't move, you tell yourself. Whatever you do, don't run. No quick movements.

But do you really want to stand there and be eaten alive? Especially when there could be water down in that pit!

Your mind races, trying to think quickly.

Two ideas come to you. You could throw some of the Fruity Bites to the crocodile. Then maybe it would leave you alone.

Or you could try moving very, very slowly past him on the stairs. If you don't find water, you might need those Fruity Bites.

What will you do?

If you throw the croc some Fruity Bites, turn to PAGE 116.

If you try to move past him, turn to PAGE 87.

The hotel, you decide. You've got to get back there to your family. You need help!

But what if your parents take one look at you and freak out? What if they don't recognize you?

You've got to take that chance.

You tiptoe across the marble floor of the lobby. Your footsteps don't make a sound. Probably because the bandages are still wrapped round your feet.

You sneak past the still-sleeping guard and slip out into the foggy night. Your bandages trail behind you as you head back towards the hotel. You glance round, hoping no one will see you.

At the corner, you accidentally catch your reflection in a shop window. Your face is so hideous, you almost scream.

Stay calm, you tell yourself. Only one more block to go.

Uh-oh. Here comes a car.

Quick—hide!—on PAGE 29.

The mummy begins to lower the heavy lid.

"Wait!" you cry, sitting up quickly in the sarcophagus so he can't shut it. "Isn't there anything else you want? Besides coming back to life, I mean?"

After a moment, the mummy lifts his dried, bony hand to his face and strokes his cheek. A few prunelike fingers jut out from beneath his bandages.

"I ... want ... to ... look ... younger," the mummy whispers. "My ... skin ... is ... so ... dry."

Younger? you think. Is he nuts?

Yes.

But hey! This is California, right? Everyone wants to look younger here!

There's only one problem. How can you make a four-thousand-year-old *mummy* look younger?

Find out on PAGE 11.

What is this place? you wonder. It certainly doesn't look like the basement of a modern skyscraper.

Why can't you see any big basement equipment, like boilers and furnaces and things?

Where's the caretaker, anyway?

The sound of your footsteps bounces off the stone walls. The echo makes the back of your neck tingle.

The hallway narrows. You duck in some places to avoid banging into the ceiling. The path twists and turns, sometimes sloping up, sometimes down.

There's barely enough light for you to see. You worry that you won't find your way back.

Maybe this is a mistake . . .

But you keep going. Except for the eerie silence and the darkness, this place is cool. You're too curious to turn back now. You come to a small tunnel leading off to the right. It seems to slope up.

A set of stone steps leads down on the left.

Which way?

If you take the tunnel, turn to PAGE 70.
If you take the steps, turn to PAGE 83.

50

You decide to push the mummy off the tower. It could be your only hope of returning to normal. If he is destroyed, maybe the spell will be broken!

"So long, creep!" you shout as you lunge forward and give him a hard shove.

"Aaahhghhhgh!" the mummy cries as he falls over the guard-rail. He screams the whole way down.

Down . . .

Down.

He hits the ground with a dull, smacking sound. Not a *THUD*, really. More like a *CRACK*.

"Way . . . to . . . go!" Derek cries, slowly lifting his wrapped arms to give you high fives.

"Yeah . . ." you say, trying to smile. But your face feels frozen, even stiffer than before.

Uh-oh.

Go to PAGE 100.

You'll hide as soon as you get a better look at those bandages!

Your hand shakes as you bend down to pick up a long piece of cloth. It's so old and thin and gauzy.

Can this really be a bandage that wrapped up the mummy?

Almost in a trance, you stare at the ancient fabric in your hands. Your eyes glaze over. All you can think about is the mummy . . .

Out there . . . somewhere . . . alive.

When you snap out of the day-dream, you hear the footsteps again. You glance up and peer into the dark corners of the lobby.

You spot a shadow moving.

Uh-oh! Time to hide! You try to drop the cloth, but for some reason, you can't seem to let go. You glance down and gasp!

Somehow, the bandage has wrapped itself round your hand!

And round your arm.

It's wrapping up your whole body!

Turn to PAGE 69.

Nope. You haven't lost them.

Two men are still following you. On donkeys. You can see them clearly now. One of them is dressed in a black suit, black shirt and white tie. Like an American gangster. The other is wearing a long, Arab-style robe.

What do they want? Why won't they leave you alone?

You ride deeper into the desert, trying to escape.

The hot sun bears down on you. But as night falls, the temperature drops to below zero. You shiver and your teeth chatter. But you keep riding.

"Give up!" the Arab man calls to you from his donkey.

"Never," you shout back. "Never!"

"You asked for it," the American gangster yells.

With that, he rides up beside your camel, leaps at you, and knocks you to the ground. Then he grabs the lead-rope for your camel, climbs back on to his donkey, and rides off.

Leaving you for the buzzards.

All that for a camel? That's all they wanted? You never knew that camels were so valuable! Suppose now you do. Now that you're stuck without one in the middle of the desert.

You've been ripped off twice today. Don't you think that's enough? Maybe you should just start again. And keep your eyes open this time!

THE END

You stumble as the mummy drags you down the hotel hallway. He leads you out of a side service entrance.

Fog floats in the darkness, just above the street lamps. The back alley is empty, except for a rat that scampers away when it hears you coming.

Once you're outside, you reckon it's time to make a break for it. "Let me go!" you cry. You try to pull away from the mummy, but you can't. His hold on your wrist is powerful. His grip is like a steel vice.

"Come ... on ..." he rasps in his breathy whisper. "We've ... got ... to ... hurry."

Hurry? Where?

Quickly, the mummy brings you back to the Pyramid Building. No one sees you sneak back into the lobby of the building. Not even the guard, who is still asleep.

Silently, the mummy pulls you towards the sarcophagus that was his resting-place for four thousand years. Shattered glass is still scattered all around.

"Get ... in!" the mummy orders you, pointing to it.

Get *in*? Into a sarcophagus?

If you get into the mummy case, turn to PAGE 68.

If you try to escape again, turn to PAGE 21.

You decide to ask Illinois Smith for help.

Why not? He's always working out ancient curses and translating foreign languages and things like that in his films.

"Uh, excuse me," you say, walking up to Smith.

Actually, his real name's not Smith. That's just his character's name. But you can't remember his real name.

"Yeah?" he says, glancing at you from under his famous brown hat.

You hand him the strange thin pages of the mummy's diary. "Uh, I was wondering if you could—"

But before you can finish your sentence, Smith grabs the diary out of your hands. "Sure, kid," he says. "Any time."

Then he pulls out a big, fat, felt-tipped marker and scrawls an autograph across the page, completely blotting out the ancient writing underneath!

Did you really think a *film* star was going to decipher hieroglyphics for you?

Really?

Well, decipher this: Ha. Ha-ha-ha. Hah-hah-hah-hah!

THE END

Suddenly you hear the boot of the car open. Someone's lifting you out! Your stiff mummified body slides forwards in the wooden sarcophagus. You bang your head.

Ow! you think.

"Hurry up!" George whispers loudly. "The boat's about to leave! Help me get this heavy coffin on board."

On board! you think. Where are they taking me?

BUMP. SLAM. OOOMPH.

Your body crashes against the walls of the mummy case, slapping first to one side and then the other. Owwww . . .

Suddenly, you begin to feel dizzy. Light-headed. Strange all over. What's going on?

Maybe all this slamming around is getting to me, you think.

"Put it down there," a deep voice suddenly commands. "Let's see this living mummy you've told me about."

It's a new voice. Someone you haven't heard before.

KA-BUMP. The two guards drop the sarcophagus with a heavy thud. Then someone lifts the lid and peers inside. Light streams in on you.

"Hey! What's happening to him?" the man with the deep voice cries. "He smells rotten!"

Turn to PAGE 13.

You press the UP button five more times. Finally you hear the familiar *DING*—the sound that means the lift has arrived. The doors open.

Oh, no!

A scream rises in your throat. But it never escapes.

And neither will you.

There, standing in the lift is your old friend, the mummy.

Your *very* old friend.

The mummy was mad when you stole his diary. But that was nothing compared to how he feels now. He hates trespassers. And you dared to enter his sacred burial chamber. Uninvited.

Your visit to his tomb is about to come to a very unpleasant end. And so are you.

When the mummy has finished with you, you're going to need all those mummy bandages!

THE END

With a horrible clatter of plates, glasses and cutlery, the hotel room-service waiter crashes to the floor.

Whimpering, he gazes at you from the floor with a bowl of strawberry ice-cream melting on his chest. Pieces of club sandwich decorate his shoulders. A big blob of mayonnaise drips from his ear.

"What did you do that for?" he asks, moaning in pain.

You glance at his right arm. It's wrapped up in bandages.

"Oops," you say. You gulp. Your face turns bright red. "I thought you were a mummy."

"A mummy?" the waiter repeats. He shakes his head. "Man, this hasn't been my day. First, I cut my hand and now this!" He moans again. "Ohhhhhh. I think my leg is broken."

"What's going on?" your mother demands from the bedroom door.

"It—it was an accident, Mum," you sputter.

Then you start apologizing—fast. To your parents. To the waiter. To your parents, again. And even to Susie, for waking her up. Everybody's mad at you. Everybody except for one person. Derek. And he can't stop laughing.

Turn to PAGE 34 to find out why.

An ancient smiley face? That's a good one! You decide it's a bunch of birds sitting round a camp-fire. They look like they're having a good time, too.

But what does it mean? you wonder. Nobody's there to answer you.

Sand swirls round you. Your throat is so hot and dry, you can hardly swallow. You have to find some water.

The best you can do is keep walking. And so you do. You walk and walk and walk.

Twenty minutes. Thirty. Still no water.

But then you see something else. Something you recognize.

The Sphinx! A huge stone monument in the desert, near the pyramids. The Sphinx has the body of a lion, with a human head.

Eagerly, you run the thirty or so metres to the stone monument. She towers over you, more than twenty metres tall.

Wow, you think, gazing up at the Sphinx. There's something eerie and mysterious about her. She looks as if she knows a secret and won't tell.

Suddenly, you hear a voice. A huge booming voice, coming from the giant statue.

"Go back," the Sphinx commands you. "You must not trespass on the graves of kings!"

Turn to PAGE 119.

Ten minutes go by. Twenty.

You stand in the storage cupboard. Hiding. Waiting for someone to find you.

But who will it be?

You hate this part. It feels too much like playing hide-and-seek. Waiting to be caught.

Suddenly you hear footsteps in the hall. Quiet footsteps.

You hold your breath.

The footsteps stop right outside the storage cupboard door.

Silence.

Why doesn't he come in? you wonder. What's he waiting for?

Is it Derek?

You don't dare open the door. What if it's not Derek? What if it's someone else?

Silence.

Finally you start to reach for the doorknob. Before you touch it, it turns by itself. The door swings open.

No!

You—your body, your face—you're standing out in the hall!

But it isn't you. It's the mummy, inside your body.

Quickly he reaches out and grabs you by the neck!

Turn to PAGE 42.

Your hand trembles as you turn page after page. They're all the same. All hieroglyphs!

Terror grips your heart. How can the diary be written in hieroglyphics? Have you somehow gone back in time? On top of everything else?

You glance round and see some people in modern clothes.

Okay, you reassure yourself. At least I'm still in the present.

You may still have a chance at getting back home.

And you want to get there right now!

You turn sharply and head back towards the steps. But a young Egyptian man in a long, white robe blocks your way. He has smooth, tanned skin, black hair and sparkling brown eyes. You notice he's wearing a badge. He must be some kind of security guard.

"No entrance," he says in English.

"But I just came out of there!" you sputter.

"No entrance," he says. "The Great Pyramid is not open."

Turn to PAGE 128.

You decide Derek is right. You can't let the mummy have the diary. It seems really creepy to fool around with magic, especially magic that brings someone back to life who's been dead four thousand years!

"No deal," you tell the mummy. Then, just to be sure he doesn't grab the diary away from you, you rip it to shreds.

He stares at you with his hollow eye sockets. It gives you chills.

Uh-oh. Now he's mad. Really mad.

"Then ... I ... must ... seek ... my ... revenge," the mummy says, letting each word escape between wheezing breaths.

The mummy's hand darts out. He grabs your wrist. He's unbelievably strong!

"You ... must ... come ... with ... me," he says, dragging you towards the hall. "Or ..."

Or? You have a choice?

"Or ... let ... me ... have ... that ... child."

With the last word, the mummy lets go of your wrist and points to your little sister who's still asleep on the sofa.

Hmmm ...

Should you go with the mummy on PAGE 6?
Or should you let the mummy take Susie on PAGE 64?

Your heart pounds faster and faster. The diary was true! But how? How can an ancient mummy come back to life?

The mummy is taller than you had expected. And bulkier, too. In fact, he seems to be nearly two metres tall, and he's built more like a football player than a dead king.

He could flatten me with one hand, you think.

SCRAPE ... SCRAPE ...

He's coming closer.

SCRAPE ... SCRAPE ...

He's bigger than his mummy case, you realize. But how can that be? Did he grow larger when he came back to life?

Better stop wondering and start worrying! You've been so fascinated by the mummy, you've forgotten that if you can see him, he can probably see you!

You pop your head back behind the pillar.

Now what?

You are hiding from a huge, living mummy in the middle of the night with no one around to help you. Running away seems like an excellent idea.

But as soon as you take a step past the pillar, two bandaged hands wrap round your throat!

Turn to PAGE 78.

Two *thousand* dollars? For an old book you found on the floor? That sounds *great* to you!

"It's a deal, then," Web declares, his eyes twinkling. "I only have one hundred dollars on me now. But I can get the rest by this afternoon."

He pulls a hundred dollars out of his pocket and hands it to you. You like this man!

"Meet me in the Mouski—the old shopping bazaar—in two hours. I'll give you the rest of the money then. And in the meantime, I'll take the diary with me for safe keeping."

"Uh, I don't know about *that*," you start to say. But before you can stop him, Web grabs the diary and slips it into his briefcase. Then he quickly walks out of the cafe and disappears into the crowd.

He doesn't even wait for the lemonade.

Turn to PAGE 74.

"Take her—not me!" you shout.

What?

You're going to let a revenge-crazed mummy take your innocent little sister away? Just to save yourself?

What kind of a creep are you? You should be ashamed!

"You . . . are . . . a . . . jerk," the mummy whispers at you as he carries Susie out of the door.

See? Even the mummy thinks you did the wrong thing!

"Ah, who cares," Derek says when they've gone. "She was a little pest anyway."

Yeah, maybe. But guess what? Your little pest of a sister was smarter than you thought. She was only *pretending* to be asleep. When you weren't looking, she grabbed the pieces of the mummy's diary right out from under you. She slipped them under her nightgown and took them with her. Then she helped the mummy tape it back together and work out how to come back to life.

And guess what else? Once the mummy was human again, he became famous. So did Susie. And he was so grateful to her that he showered her with gifts, jewels and a small kingdom. Not to mention her big motion-picture deal in Hollywood.

And she's not even going to let you play yourself in the film. So there!

THE END

The light from your torch is dwindling. It's going to burn out soon.

Quick! Memorize the map and the path you need to take to reach the lift. Remember—you're in the tomb right now. When you come out of the tomb, you'll need to make a choice at the first fork in the passageway.

Which way? Right or left?

Then you'll have to make three more choices at forks or crossroads.

Right or left?

Don't worry about the places where the hallway simply bends or turns. You'll just follow it then. Your only problem is choosing what to do when you reach a fork in the path.

You've got to memorize all four choices, because when the torch burns out, you'll be walking in the dark.

So do it now.

Which way to the lift from the tomb?

Should you go left, then right, then right, then straight? If so, turn to PAGE 127.

Or should you go left, then right, then left, then right? If so, turn to PAGE 109.

Standing in the doorway in front of you is the most terrifying thing you've ever seen in your life.

You!

At least, it *looks* like you. You know that it's really the mummy. He stole your body, and now he's living in your hotel room. And wearing your clothes!

He looks really stupid in your pyjamas, too.

The mummy—the kid who looks like you—laughs in your face.

Then he slams the door. And double locks it.

Hey—! you try to shout. But no sound comes out.

That's when you realize—

You can't speak!

Turn to PAGE 75.

You toss a coin. It comes up heads.

Or it would have come up heads. Unfortunately, the coin that George flipped was one of those tricky two-sided coins. Both sides were tails. It didn't have a "heads" side!

Of course! That's why he was so eager to toss a coin in the first place!

Which means you're out of luck.

If you want to continue reading this story, keep tossing a coin until it comes up tails.
Then turn to PAGE 17.

68

Your throat tightens in terror as the mummy points to his sarcophagus and repeats the words.

"Get . . . in."

No way do you want to do it. Lie down in a musty old box? Where a mummy lay dead for centuries? Where you may be locked for eternity? The thought is horrifying.

But what choice do you have? Derek isn't going to show up now. He's still back at the hotel, frozen stiff. Frozen by some ancient magic the mummy used.

If I don't get in, the mummy will point his finger and freeze me, too, you think.

You lift one leg and then the other, climbing into the small, gold-encrusted wooden box. The mummy case is carved in the shape of a human being.

A shiver runs through you as you lie down. How come you fit so snugly into the mummy sarcophagus? How come it feels as if it were made just for you? Is this more mummy magic?

And how long will you have to stay in there? Will you be able to breathe? Is the mummy going to bury you *alive*?

The mummy lifts the heavy wooden lid and begins to lower it. In an instant, you will be sealed inside this airless box—possibly for ever! You've got to do something!

Turn to PAGE 72.

Terrified, you claw the bandages with both hands. You tear at them, trying to pull them away from your arms, your neck . . .

But by now your hands are wrapped up. Both of them. It's as if you're wearing gauze mittens. You can't grip the cloth. The harder you try to pull the bandages away, the more tightly they encircle you.

You gaze down at your legs. Oh, no! They're wrapped up, too. In fact, your whole body is completely bandaged.

Like a mummy!

No! you want to scream. But the sound won't come out.

Then you hear a scuffling sound again. An instant later, a figure steps out of the shadows.

You gasp and stumble back.

It's the mummy!

You stare in horror at his brown and leathery, dried, shrunken body.

Then he starts to walk towards you.

Find out what he wants on PAGE 82.

You decide to explore the tunnel. You step into it and start to climb up its gentle slope.

Almost immediately, you feel a draught. There's a weird chill in the air. Where is it coming from? Maybe the tunnel leads directly outside, you think.

But then the tunnel twists sharply and starts sloping downwards.

You keep walking even though the light is getting dimmer. You've gone this far. Might as well discover where it leads.

A few more steps downwards and—ouch!— your shoulders scrape against the walls.

The tunnel's getting even narrower, you notice. In fact, soon enough the tunnel is so narrow, you have to turn sideways to fit through.

And what's that funny smell? It smells like burning rubber or something. It makes your nose tingle and your throat feel tight.

Suddenly, exploring doesn't seem like such a good idea. In fact, you're beginning to think it's all a big mistake.

But you hate to chicken out of an adventure. And how dangerous can the basement of an office building be?

If you keep going, turn to PAGE 93.
If you turn back, scurry to the stone steps on PAGE 83.

The officer places your dad in handcuffs! Your family just stands there looking stunned.

"You people must be crazy!" one policeman says. "Vandalizing a priceless Egyptian exhibit like that. We got a call earlier tonight about a stolen mummy, but I didn't think we'd find it this fast!"

Your little sister starts to cry.

Derek shouts, "Wait! Wait! You're making a mistake!"

But the weirdest part of it all is what the mummy does. He starts to laugh!

It's as if he can't help it. He laughs and laughs and laughs. He can't stop. And it doesn't sound like your laugh, either. It's more like an evil cackle! Even the policemen look at him strangely.

Your mum looks down at you lying still on the floor. And she smiles! She smiles right at you.

You stand up with a start and run behind her.

The officers both gasp! One reaches for his gun! But your mum grabs his arm with her hand and stops him.

"Don't you dare!" she shouts. "That's my boy you're after!"

Now it's the mummy's turn to look stunned. Your mum recognizes you! And that's when you finally know you're in for a happy

ENDING.

"Help!" you cry out, trying to wake the guard. "Someone—help me!"

The mummy's dead eye sockets stare at you coldly as he starts to bring the lid into place.

"Wait!" you cry. "I can help you." Your mind races with ideas, trying to think of some way— any way—to save yourself. Then it hits you.

"Even without the diary, I can bring you back to life," you say.

For a very long moment, the mummy just stares. His wheezing breaths are the only sounds that echo in the marble lobby. Will he believe you?

"You . . . can?" he finally asks.

"Yes!" you declare firmly.

Well, you can on one condition. If you've read the GOOSEBUMPS book *Return of the Mummy*—and if you can remember the secret chant that brought *that* mummy back to life!

Think hard. Your life depends on it!

If you think it was "Klatu Barrada Nicto", *turn to PAGE 32.*

If you think it was "Teki Kahru Teki Kahra Teki Khari", *turn to PAGE 37.*

Your heart starts to pound. You don't want to go into the tomb first. You're not even sure you want to go in at all.

"Uh, why are we doing this again?" you ask Mohammed. "Remind me."

Mohammed brings his face very close to yours, nose to nose.

"Because if you don't," he says, "the mummy will rise from his coffin in San Francisco and stalk you, day and night. Everywhere you turn, you'll see his wrinkled skin, his hollow, screaming eyes. You'll hear echoes of the tortured cries he screamed as the high priestess wrapped him in bandages and buried him alive. He'll haunt your day-dreams, too. And fill your nightmares. You won't be able to think a single thought without picturing him in his moment of death. You'll know his agony when—"

"Okay! Okay! That's enough!" you say, suddenly interrupting him. "What do you want me to do?"

"Go in," Mohammed says, and he points to the tomb.

Enter the tomb on PAGE 15.

Two hours later, you take a taxi to the Mouski. It's an ancient part of Cairo—an open-air bazaar filled with traders and craftsmen selling gold, gems, silk, spices, ivory and perfume.

How is Web going to find you in this crowd? you wonder.

You wait, growing hotter and more nervous every minute. You didn't like the way Web disappeared with the diary earlier. And you don't like the way the high Egyptian sun beats down on you.

One hour . . . two hours . . .

By late afternoon, the truth sinks in. You've been set up. Web's not coming. He stole your diary and this whole "meet-me-in-the-bazaar" thing was a trick!

Bummer.

Well at least you made a hundred dollars out of the deal. That will certainly pay for a call home. You glance round, trying to figure out where you can make an international phone call. Suddenly an Arab man approaches you, leading a camel.

"Here," he mutters in a low voice with a thick accent. "Take this camel and go! Your life is in great danger!"

Hurry to PAGE 39.

For a moment, you stand in the hallway just staring at the locked door.

Locked.

Locked out of your hotel room.

Locked away from your family.

Locked out of your own life.

And no one even knows it! you realize. Your family probably thinks the mummy is you!

Why not? He looks like you . . .

"No!" you want to cry. "You can't steal my life that way!"

But your mouth won't make a sound.

Suddenly, you hear a noise. The lift. Someone's coming.

Your heart pounds faster.

Don't let anyone see me, you think. Please.

Quick—hide on PAGE 10.

76

"What have you done to my brother?" you shriek.

The mummy doesn't answer you. He simply takes another wheezing breath.

Terrified, you struggle to lift your hands to your face. You can barely move. You want to scream again when you see your fingers. They're bony, brown, shrivelled and dry—just like the mummy's. Just like Derek's.

Finally you touch your own cheeks and feel for your eyes. Your fingers probe the spots where your eyes used to be.

"NO!" you scream as you plunge your fingers into the deep, empty holes of your eye sockets.

Your eyes have gone!

But how can that be? you wonder. You can still see.

But before you can speak again, the whole world seems to go black. Suddenly you can see nothing. Hear nothing. Feel nothing—except a terrible dizzying whirl.

Turn to PAGE 107.

Nooooooo! Unwrapping the bandages didn't work! You're still a mummy.

Your screams are so loud, they awaken the sleeping guard. The one who's been snoring at his desk until now.

Startled, he whips round and lumbers over to where you're standing.

"Yeowww-sa!" the guard cries out. "What the—?"

The guard is a pot-bellied man with red veins on his nose.

Instantly, he reaches towards the side of his belt, to the place where a holster would be.

No, you think. Please don't shoot me. I don't want to die!

You start to duck. But he pulls out a walkie-talkie instead of a gun. He pushes the button and speaks into it.

"George? Come quick! We've got trouble!" the guard shouts.

Then he moves towards you. He looks a bit scared. He raises his fists.

"No wait!" you try to say. "I'm just a kid!"

Your lips form the words but your voice doesn't work. No sound comes out.

You can't talk!

Go on to PAGE 113.

"Don't!" you cry out, although the mummy is nearly choking you and you can hardly breathe. The sound of your voice is muffled, tiny. Not even loud enough to wake the guard.

The mummy lifts you off the ground by the throat. You clutch at his bandaged hands, trying to pull them off your neck. His grip relaxes just enough to allow you to breathe.

But he doesn't let go.

You stare into his eyes. They seem hollow, empty. Dead.

Then he opens his mouth.

Is he going to speak?

What will the ancient king say to you?

Find out on PAGE 121.

You decide to take the passageway to the right.

At the end of the hall, you come to a large, square burial chamber. Inside, by the light from Mohammed's torch, you see a stone platform where the mummy's coffin once rested. Now the mummy is in San Francisco, on display. But other special objects that once belonged to King Buthramaman are still there.

"So this is the mummy's tomb?" you ask quietly. Mohammed nods.

"Hey—what's that?" you ask. You spot a hinged wooden box shaped like a serpent and painted gold.

"That is where the diary belongs," Mohammed says. "Place it there."

He's right. The diary fits in the box perfectly.

"Now I must leave you," Mohammed says. "It is forbidden for me to stay in the king's tomb. But I'll give you this map and a small torch." He hands them to you. "The light should last long enough for you to study the map. If you make the right choices, you will find your way back through the mystical portal to your land. It was the mummy's magic that brought you here, and the same magic can take you back. Good luck."

"Wait!" you cry.

But you are too late. Mohammed has bolted from the chamber.

Turn to PAGE 108.

80

The police? Your parents are calling the police—to have them take you away?

Your heart races, panicked at the thought.

You know what's going to happen next. A load of museum people will drag you away and study you. Or scientists from the government. They'll lock you up. Stick things in you. Maybe even cut you open!

Mum! Dad! you silently cry. Don't you know it's me?

Suddenly you get an idea.

You relax your arms and play dead. Really dead, like a mummy is supposed to be.

Every muscle in your body goes limp.

You just lie perfectly still on the floor, hardly breathing.

The police burst through the door a few moments later. They find a normal-looking family huddled round a motionless Egyptian mummy.

"A living mummy! Yeah, that's a new one," you hear one of the officers say. "Does he look alive to you?"

The other officer chuckles. "Yeah, I've heard some good ones in my time, but that's a first." Then he adds, "All right, put 'em up!"

The policeman is walking towards your dad with handcuffs!

Turn to PAGE 71.

Forget him, you decide. He's just a film character. What would he know about hieroglyphics in real life?

Besides, beyond the film set you can see a catering truck!

They'd have something to drink!

A moment later you're sitting in the shade of one of the pyramids with a cool, refreshing bottle of cola.

You pull the diary out of your pocket again and study the pictures in the book.

There's the page with the birds, page 7. And there's another with fish. You notice that each of the pages has one, two, or three stars in the corner.

One of the extras from the film sits down next to you. He peers over your shoulder, noticing the ancient-looking book in your hand.

"Hey," he says, pointing to the page with birds on it. "That restaurant's still in downtown Cairo. Pete's Chicken Grill. Best place in town."

Restaurant? Chicken Grill? What's he talking about?

Then it dawns on you. The picture of birds and fish. The stars in the corner. The diary is a restaurant guide! Who'd have thought Buthramaman was really the world's first restaurant critic!

Oh, well, don't feel bad. You've solved the mystery of the mummy's diary. And now you know where to get a good meal.

THE END

82

This can't be happening! your brain screams. The diary *can't* be true! A mummy can't come back to life. Not after being dead for four thousand years.

But he is! And he is coming straight towards you!

His nose is a pointed bump on his hard, brown-leather face. His eye sockets have no eyeballs. They're just big, gaping pits. His mouth is open in a hideous half-smile, half-scream.

He's so tiny, you think. About your height, but much thinner. Bonier. So horrible, but so small.

For just an instant, you feel sorry for him.

Until you realize he's coming closer ... closer ...

Before you know it, he reaches out and touches your face.

A sudden jolt flows through you—like an electrical shock. Then the mummy pulls his hand away. Your heart nearly stops as you watch what's happening.

The mummy begins to transform.

Into you!

Try to stop trembling as you turn to PAGE 94.

You decide to take the stone steps to the left. The narrow tunnel gives you the creeps.

After a few steps down, the stairs level out. You see another set of steps leading upwards. You start to climb again.

Your feet scrape across something gritty on the floor. You glance down and see sand.

Sand?

Definitely weird, you think as you reach another stone landing. You feel as if you've been climbing up and down for days. You stretch your legs, and then continue up the stairs.

Where do the steps come out? you wonder. A back exit from the Pyramid Building? Do they lead into another building?

A hot breeze ruffles your hair as you near the top of the steps.

That's odd, you think. It was chilly this morning. And the weatherperson on TV predicted rain.

Finally, you reach the top. You walk outside and squint as your eyes adjust to the brilliant sun.

"Huh?" Your mouth drops open as you gaze at the scene in front of you.

Sand? Camels? Pyramids? Desert?

Is this—? No, it can't be. Are you in Egypt?

Turn to PAGE 95.

The mummy's angry voice terrifies you.

"Close ... the ... lid!" he shouts, his voice booming.

Shaking, you do as he says, shutting him into the mummy case. Then you begin to recite the ancient words.

"*Teki Kahru Teki Kahra Teki Khari*," you say, your voice trembling. That's one. "*Teki Kahru Teki Kahra Teki Khari*."

That's two.

You say it a third time. But now your voice is steadier. You concentrate hard, making sure the words are recited in the right order. "*Teki Kahru Teki Kahra Teki Khari*."

Then a fourth. "*Teki Kahru Teki Kahra Teki Khari*."

You take a deep breath. One more time and the mummy will come back to life. You hesitate and swallow hard.

Do I really want to do this? you wonder. What about Derek's warning? What about not playing around with dead people? Why not just walk away and leave the mummy lying there, trapped again in his closed case?

Think about it as you turn to PAGE 25.

You take a sip of the lemonade.

Are you *nuts*?

Blue lemonade? I mean, come on! Whoever heard of *blue* lemonade?

It could be poison! It could be sleeping pills!

This is terrible. You shouldn't be wandering loose in Egypt if you can't be more careful than that.

Well—no problem. You're not loose in Egypt any more.

You're out cold!

Because whatever was in that lemonade has put you instantly to sleep. And when you wake up, the diary has gone.

Of course, without the diary, you have no business being in this book. So close it immediately. And when you open it again, try to be more careful. Please!

THE END

"Reallllly?" the other doctor says slowly. "A *living* mummy?" He steps forward and peers at you over the top of his gold wire-rimmed glasses. "Amazing!"

"I sure would like to see what's inside this guy," the female doctor says. "Wouldn't you?"

The male doctor nods and grins. "We could make a lot of money on this," he mutters.

You don't like the way these two are looking at you. There's something creepy about the glint in their eyes. And the eager expressions on their faces.

And what does she mean—see what's inside? One thing's for sure: it doesn't sound good!

The female doctor tightens her grip on your wrist.

You glance back out to the street to see if the limousine has gone. It hasn't.

What are you going to do?

If you pull away and dash out into the street, turn to PAGE 91.

If you stay hidden in the alcove with the doctors, turn to PAGE 112.

Water, you say to yourself. I desperately need water.

It's all you can think about. If there's water in that pit, then you've got to get down there.

So, moving as slowly as you can, you step past the croc.

Big mistake.

Because the crocodile was saying to himself, Lunch. I desperately need lunch.

Too bad for you. No water. No treasure. No escape from the croc. Looks like Buthramaman's treasure is fool's gold. And guess who the fool is?

THE END

I'm getting out of here, you decide. Running into a mummy *or* a guard would probably be bad news.

You race through the revolving door at the front of the lobby. You run down the dark, empty streets towards your hotel.

Hey—are those footsteps behind you?

You don't look back. You don't *want* to know if the mummy is behind you!

Finally you reach your hotel room and slip inside with your key.

Phew, you think. Safe.

Luckily, everyone is still asleep. Your parents' door is closed, so they don't even hear you come in.

The room is really a suite. Your parents are sleeping in the bedroom and you, Derek and Susie have the living-room. A thin blade of light streams into the living-room from the bathroom. The light has been left on for Susie, who is snoring on the sofa. Derek is stretched out on a camp-bed.

You tiptoe past him, heading towards your sleeping-bag on the floor.

Suddenly a hand reaches out and grabs your arm!

Turn to PAGE 131.

Marvin nods towards the corner of the room. For the first time you look round. You're in a huge museum storage room. And there are other mummies, too! Not far from you. They're lying on tables in the far corner.

"The others are always saying the same thing," Marvin explains. "Pretending they have families to get to. I can't leave them alone for a minute. They'd try to escape. And I wouldn't be a very good museum director if I let all my mummies go, would I?"

What's he talking about? Are the other mummies alive, too? Is he not going to let you go?

"You're an important artifact from ancient Egypt," he adds. "A major addition to our collection. You'll understand if I have to keep you under lock and key."

He's carrying you over to a storage locker! A big one in the far corner. He's putting you in it! Wait a minute. You thought he was going to help!

You move your hand up and down like mad. Pretending to write. Hoping he'll give you the pencil and paper again!

"Don't worry," he adds as he swings the locker door shut. "You'll get to see your family again someday—we'll send them tickets to the exhibition!"

THE END

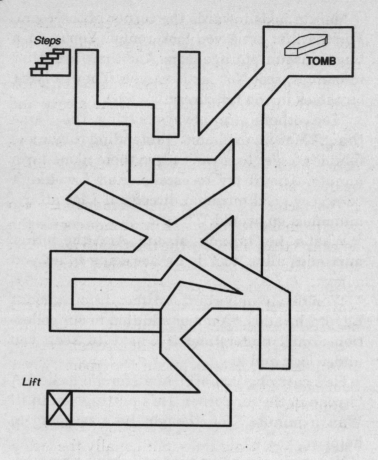

Keep your finger on this page so you can study the map. But turn to PAGE 65.

These doctors are creeps, you decide. They're looking at you as if they've just won the lottery—and you're the prize!

You've got to get away from them. You yank your wrist hard. You dash out of the alcove and back on to the pavement.

Luckily, the limousine driver doesn't seem to notice you. Even with your bandages trailing behind you.

The doctors chase you, but you manage to slip away from them. You sneak into a side door of the hotel and take the lift to the thirteenth floor. You rush to the room you share with your family.

Then you reach for your room key. Your heart starts to pound. Oh, no! You forgot. You're a mummy! No pockets, no room key.

You knock on the door. What else can you do?

You hear footsteps inside the room. Good. Someone's coming.

But who?

You hope it's your older brother, Derek. He can be a jerk sometimes, but usually the two of you get along.

You wrap your face back up as best you can and put your hand on your hip—trying to look casual.

The door swings open.

When you see who's there, a scream rises in your throat.

Who's at the door? Find out on PAGE 66.

Before you know it, Derek and your dad rush forward and grab your arms. Roughly, they wrestle you to the floor.

"No, Dad. It's me!" you want to scream.

But it's Susie who does the screaming. You glance at your mother, hoping that at least she will recognize you. Your own mother!

But her eyes grow wide with fear. She reaches out and yanks Susie towards her. She hugs your little sister close to protect her. From you!

You'd never hurt your own sister!

You struggle to get up, but Derek sits on your legs. Your dad holds your arms.

You flail around and pull one arm free—just for an instant. With a gauzy finger, you point accusingly at the mummy. Then you point at yourself, tapping your own chest. Then you point back at the mummy again.

Will they get it? Will your parents see what you're trying to tell them? That the mummy is not really you? And you aren't really the mummy?

For just an instant, they seem to understand.

Go on to PAGE 102.

Hey—good for you! You've got a great spirit of adventure.

There's only one pitfall with that kind of attitude. You never know when you're going to stumble into something bad.

Did we say pitfall?

Did we say stumble?

You take two more steps and your foot suddenly gets caught in a small crack in the floor. You stumble forwards—and fall.

"Aaahhhhh!" you scream as you find yourself falling.

Falling . . . falling . . . into a pit thirty metres deep!

You finally land on the bottom. At least you land on something soft. But then you start to sink.

Thick warm ooze covers your body, sucking you under. The ooze grows warmer and warmer. Now it's burning hot, scorching your skin.

You realize the ooze is tar—burning hot tar!

You've learnt about tar pits at school. That's where archaeologists have found the remains of cavemen and dinosaurs. The hot tar coats the body and preserves the bones.

Congratulations! You're saved . . . for the next thousand years at least!

THE END

The mummy's leathery face softens and then fills out. His dried skin becomes fleshy and alive.

Hey! That's *your* face! Not only that, he's even wearing your clothes!

Then he turns and runs away.

Your face and body start to tingle. Something's happening. Something horrible!

You grab and claw at the bandages that wrap you tightly. Under the bandages, you can feel your flesh shrivelling and drying—as if you've been sitting in an oven for four thousand years.

It's the bandages, you realize. The bandages are doing something to your skin!

You notice a loose end of cloth dangling from a long bandage. You yank it and the cloth round your head begins to unwind.

You have to see what's happened to you! You race towards the lifts, frantically unwrapping as you go. You gaze into the polished chrome lift doors.

No!

Your heart pounds in terror when you see your reflection.

Your face! It's brown and leathery. Your skin is dried and shrunken. Your mouth is a gaping hole.

You've turned into the mummy!

Turn to PAGE 103.

No way, you think, shaking your head. This can't be happening. It isn't real.

How can I be in Egypt? you wonder. How?

Stay calm, you tell yourself over and over. You've just come out of the Pyramid Building in San Francisco. In the United States of America. You *can't* be in Egypt!

But you are. You see the pyramids and the camels. You hear the wind blowing across the desert. You feel the sand in your eyes. You can even smell and taste a sweet, flowery fragrance in the air.

You swallow hard and try to work out how . . . why . . .

Suddenly it hits you. The diary. This must have something to do with the mummy's diary!

You yank the ancient pages out from under your shirt and open the diary again.

The words you read just a few minutes ago have gone.

Instead, the whole diary is filled with symbols and pictures.

Hieroglyphics!

Go back to PAGE 60.

"I know what you're thinking," Derek says. "It's weird that the mummy disappeared last night, just like I wrote in the diary. It must be some freaky coincidence."

"Yeah," you agree weakly. "I suppose so."

But you're not one hundred per cent sure.

Still, you feel a lot better knowing that it was all a big joke, even if you do feel stupid. At least there isn't a mad mummy after you, trying to get revenge.

You do a lot of great things for the rest of your holiday. You ride in a cable car, then visit Golden Gate Park. You even take a ferry to Alcatraz, the island prison.

It isn't until you get back home that you finally see the headlines in the paper: FBI NABS MUMMY-NAPPERS, RESTORES 4000-YEAR-OLD MUMMY TO SAN FRANCISCO OFFICE BUILDING.

Looks like you weren't alone in the Pyramid Building that night, after all.

THE END

Hey—you're no fool. You aren't drinking any lemonade!

"What's wrong?" Web says. "Don't you want to try your lemonade? I'm sure it's much better now that I've sweetened it for you."

You shake your head. "I'm not thirsty," you declare.

Web Woobly eyes you carefully. A huge smile spreads across his face.

"Congratulations," he says. He reaches into his jacket pocket and pulls out a wallet. When he flips it open, you see his ID card.

"I'm from the FBI," he explains. "You've passed the test. Good job! I'm happy to inform you that you've been chosen to be part of a small team of kids who are going to help us catch international art-treasure thieves."

"Huh?" you grunt. You feel really confused.

"You've passed the test!" Web repeats, gleefully. "You didn't drink that lemonade, which shows that you have good sense and great instincts. You also have a good head for negotiating for valuable art treasures, I must add."

"I do?" you ask. What's this man talking about?

Turn to PAGE 130.

Finally, all is silent.

You open your eyes.

You are all alone, standing on top of Coit Tower. You gaze at the glittering lights of the city below you. You shake your head a few times, trying to clear it.

Then you feel a hand tap you on the back.

"Thank you," a gentle voice says softly.

You whirl round to find a short, tan-skinned young man standing behind you. He wears an ancient-looking robe, trimmed in purple and gold. On his neck you see a birthmark shaped like a question mark. The birthmark that frightened his people, just as it said in the diary.

"Are you—were you—the mummy?" you ask him.

"I am the last great king of Egypt," he says, smiling shyly. "Thank you for giving me my life."

Then, before you can ask him anything else, he turns and vanishes into thin air.

"Wait!" you call out. "Come back!"

And then you see him again. At the base of the tower, far below. How did he get there so quickly? you wonder.

He strolls out into the night. You watch as his brightly-coloured robe disappears into the fog.

Turn to PAGE 124.

"An appointment?" you say. "Uh, no. But, uh, he's working for the government. He's supposed to, you know, check this place out and find out if your ads are true. Like when they say that you can make people look younger. Can you? Because if you can't, we'll have to close this place down."

"Really?" the receptionist asks nervously. "Oh—well, come on in. I'm sure we can work him in somehow."

Soon, the mummy is up to his neck in a bathtub full of green slimy stuff. A body wrap, they call it. It's supposed to make his skin young and smooth.

"Whoa!" the young woman spa attendant says to the mummy. "It's going to take more than a body wrap to get you into shape. Have you been spending a lot of time in the sun or something?"

"Yes . . ." the mummy says, wheezing between words. "It's . . . very . . . hot . . . where . . . I . . . come . . . from."

You pace up and down while the mummy has the full spa treatment. Juice drinks, steam facials, mud baths, chemical skin injections, vitamin pills, herbal teas—and a massage to top it all off.

What are the chances this is going to work? you ask yourself. And what will the mummy do if it doesn't?

Get some answers on PAGE 120.

You and Derek stare at each other in horror. "Your . . . arms!" Derek cries, pointing.

He's right. Your arms and legs are shrivelling up even more than before. Your skin is becoming harder. Drier. More prunelike. So is his.

In a matter of minutes, both you and Derek have shrunk so much that your clothes hang on you loosely. They look as if they are three sizes too big.

And you're still shrinking.

Finally, you and your brother are nothing but dust. A strong wind off the bay blows your remains all the way to Egypt. Your dust scatters through the grains of sand in front of an ancient pyramid.

This adventure has come to a dry, dusty

END.

"Get out!" Marvin yells at the guards, sending them away.

He lifts your rotting body out of the mummy case. Gently and carefully.

He grabs a handful of gauze rolls from a drawer. Then he starts wrapping you up again.

Yes! you think. The gauze feels cool and clean.

As soon as the bandages touch your skin, you begin to feel better. More alive! He's saving you!

You feel your strength return. You sit up and look Marvin in the eye.

He doesn't even flinch! It's as if he expected you to be alive.

You move your hand, pretending to write something. And he calmly hands you a pencil and paper.

"I'm a kid," you write frantically. "The mummy swapped places with me and then escaped. He stole my body! You have to help me. I have to get back to my family."

Marvin reads the note over your shoulder and sighs.

"I know," he says. "I know."

He knows! That's fantastic! you think. Maybe he knows how to change you back into a kid again!

Find out what else Marvin knows on PAGE 89.

102

You gaze into your mother's eyes. Please understand, you want to say. Please. It's me!

Your mum's mouth starts to open.

"Michael?" she whispers to your dad. "I think it's trying to tell us something."

Your dad gazes deeply into your eyes.

Does he see you in there? Or only empty eye sockets surrounded by horrible, dried, leathery flesh?

Before your dad can answer, the mummy speaks up.

"Yeah, he's telling us something. He's saying he's after me!" the mummy cries. "Like I told you!"

You see a secret twinkle in the mummy's eye. He knows the truth. He knows he's stolen your body! He knows he's telling a huge lie!

But no one else knows.

"Call the hotel security," your father declares. "Better yet, call the police."

"Yeah," the mummy gleefully agrees. "Call the police!"

Turn to PAGE 80.

The room spins. You struggle to keep from fainting.

This can't be happening!

But one more look in the chrome-mirrored lift door convinces you.

It's happening.

You're a mummy.

At first, you are too terrified to think. You just stand there in the lobby, stunned.

Then you hear the sleeping guard start to move.

Uh-oh. He's waking up.

You don't want to face him—or anyone—looking like this!

Quickly, you come up with a plan.

You've got to make it back to the hotel. Maybe your family can help. But that means walking through the streets. You'd have to take your chances and hope that no one spots you—a living mummy!

Then again, you could try to unwrap the horrible mummy bandages right now. Maybe if you get them off, you'll change back into yourself again. What should you do?

If you go back to the hotel, turn to PAGE 47.
If you unwrap yourself, turn to PAGE 115.

104

You'd better not try anything. Messing around with a mummy's spell could backfire.

The mummy opens the diary and holds it up to the sky.

"At . . . last . . . the . . . stars . . . are . . . right," the mummy says.

You glance at the page he's holding. It's a map of the stars. Then you gaze up at the sky.

"He's right!" you whisper to Derek. "Look! The stars match."

"Amazing," Derek murmurs.

"In . . . the . . . name . . . of . . . my . . . ancestors," the mummy chants, "I . . . praise . . . the . . . stars . . . and . . . all . . . that . . . shines . . . in . . . the . . . universe."

Then, to your amazement, he pulls a small vial out from under his bandages. It looks like a test-tube! Where did that come from? you wonder.

He rips the page out of the diary. He pours the liquid from the little vial on to the page . . . and eats it!

Instantly, you feel that dizzying, spinning motion. The whole world goes black as if you've closed your eyes. Then a rushing wind whips your face. Lights—or are they stars?—flash, exploding all around you.

"Derek!" you cry out. Your ears fill with a horrible wailing. Even if Derek answered, you would never hear it.

Turn to PAGE 98.

Give the mummy the diary, or else what? You are almost too afraid to wonder.

"The . . . diary!" the mummy repeats. He shakes you by the throat, making you gag. "I must . . . have . . . the . . . diary's . . . magic. That . . . is . . . the . . . only . . . way . . . I . . . can . . . return . . . to . . . life . . ."

You feel the mummy's musty hot breath on your face. It wheezes out between his hard, thin lips. Finally he lets go of your throat. You lurch away from him, but he clutches you tightly by your arm.

He's got some grip for a little dead man!

"Give him the diary!" you croak. You rub your sore throat with your free hand.

"No way," Derek says. "We can't do that."

"Why not? Are you nuts?" you yell. Then you glance towards your parents' bedroom door. "MUM! DAD!" you shout.

From behind their door, you hear your mother's sleepy voice calling back. "Go to sleep. You kids are going to be wrecks in the morning if you don't settle down."

"But, Mum!" you holler.

"Not another word!" she calls back. "Now, good-night!"

From her tone, you know she means it.

You're on your own.

The mummy tightens his grip on your arm.

Turn to PAGE 110.

106

You turn and dash away. You race across the desert sands.

You don't trust either of these men. Why should you? They're trying to take the mummy's diary away from you. The strange diary that magically changed from English to hieroglyphics.

Sand blows in your face as you leave the Great Pyramid far behind. Who cares? You'll *eat* sand, if you have to. All you want is to get out of here alive.

You try not to let the feeling of cold fear rise into your throat. You swallow hard, choking it back down.

How am I going to get home? you wonder.

And how could the diary change like that?

The diary. Maybe it contains some kind of special message. Maybe, if you can work out what the hieroglyphs mean, then you'll *know* how to get home!

You want to examine the diary again. You glance over your shoulder to make sure you're not being followed.

Are you?

Make sure.

Then turn and run to PAGE 7.

Finally the spinning stops. The darkness clears. You open your eyes and find yourself standing on top of a tower. You recognize it as Coit Tower, an old landmark in San Francisco. It's on a hill overlooking all of the city and the bay.

The long bandages that tied your wrists and attached you to the mummy have gone. But you are still wrapped in ancient cloth.

Derek is at your side. He's hideous—still a mummy with wrinkled dry skin and no eyes!

So am I, you think.

"Now ... I ... will ... come ... back ... to ... life," the mummy says as he lifts the diary and opens it. "Now ... that ... the ... stars ... are ... right. And ... I ... have ... the ... diary. And ... I ... am ... standing ... at ... the ... highest ... place ... within ... twenty ... miles."

He's only a few paces in front of you, at the edge of the tower. His back is to you as he stands facing up into the sky.

You glance down at your wrinkled hands and shudder. You don't feel so sorry for the mummy any more. Obviously, he has you under some kind of spell. How can you break his power over you?

Hmmmmmm. All it would take is one quick shove to knock the mummy off the tower. And it's a very long way down!

If you push the mummy off the tower, turn to PAGE 50.

If you wait to see him come back to life, turn to PAGE 104.

108

Mohammed runs away so fast that all you can hear is the fading sound of his sandals flip-flopping on the stone floor.

Then silence. A horrible, stone-cold silence.

You have no time to waste. The torch isn't going to last long. You hold it up and peer at the map. It's a handwritten sketch drawn on brown paper, the edges torn.

This is a *map*? This jumble of lines?

Where's the "YOU ARE HERE" sign? Your heart sinks. You need help!

But then you work it out.

The steps are those close-together lines on the top left. The tomb is the box at the end of the angled hallway.

And that other box? The one with the X in it? That's the lift! The lift in the Pyramid Building! You know, because you've seen lots of maps that are marked the same way. The lifts are always marked with X's.

And that's where you need to go, if you're ever going to get back home.

You've got a pencil in your pocket. So you take it out and write in the words "steps", "tomb" and "lift".

Then you study the map.

Turn to PAGE 90 and study the map.

You stare at the map hard and decide to turn left, then right, then left, then right.

A moment later, your torch sputters and goes out. You are stranded in the cold tomb of an ancient mummy. In the dark.

Silence.

You move a step forward, feeling your way along the wall.

Left, right, left, right, you keep telling yourself. You chant the words over and over. Left. Right. Left. Right.

Your hand brushes against something slimy.

Eeeeeewwww. You jerk your hand away.

Do you *dare* touch the wall again? You don't have a choice. How will you find your way in the dark if you don't?

Slowly, you reach one hand to the wall. Yuck. The stones are slippery with slime. You try not to think about what it might be! You hold your other hand out in front of you. You don't want to smack into anything in the dark.

Finally you come to the first fork. You turn left. Walk a little further. Turn right. A little further. Go left.

Now, if you remember the map correctly, you have just one more turn. You turn right—it should be pretty easy from now on. Keep going . . .

Turn the corner on PAGE 26.

"Derek, please! Give him the diary," you beg.

"Not until he lets you go," Derek insists.

The mummy hesitates. *WHEEZE* ... *WHEEZE* ...

Finally he releases your arm.

Your knees shake as you race to Derek's camp-bed. You reach under the mattress and yank out the mummy's diary.

"Here!" You rush towards the ancient mummy.

"Not so fast!" Derek grabs your wrist to stop you. "Listen, I know about these things. Mummies, ghosts, aliens—it's always the same. We let them loose on Earth, and we're in big trouble. I've seen it in films a lot. Helping dead people come back to life, well, it's a big mistake. Don't give him the diary. He could turn into some kind of crazy, evil monster and—"

"But Derek!" you interrupt. "He's already come back to life! What's the big deal? And anyway, he's going to *kill* me if we don't give him the diary!"

Derek shrugs. "Okay," he says. "But don't say I didn't warn you. You'll be sorry."

Derek sounds pretty sure about this. What do you think?

If you give the diary to the mummy, turn to PAGE 44.

If you think you should keep it, turn to PAGE 61.

"No!" The mummy-kid lets out a muffled cry from under his bandaged mouth.

But you ignore him. As soon as he is wrapped up, you reach out and touch him on the face. *Your* face.

Instantly, you feel a sudden jolt of electricity flow through you. Like an electrical shock. It burns and stings.

And you feel it *twice!* Once in the mummy's body. Once in your own! As if you are two people at once.

You pull your hand away.

All at once, the mummy-kid's skin begins to harden into the ancient, dried brown leather. You glance down at your own hands and watch them turn pink again!

After that, everything seems like a blur. You race to your hotel room and tell your parents the whole story. No one quite believes you about the mummy being alive, especially since he's not alive now. He seems perfectly and completely dead.

But later that night, when you pick up the mummy's diary, you find something new written on the last page.

"I am back in my prison—for now. But soon I will awaken again and take my revenge!"

Here we go again!

THE END

You decide to stay in the alcove. You don't want to risk being seen by anyone else.

Besides, you think you can get away from these doctors.

Wrong.

"Grab him, Stuart!" the female doctor suddenly shouts. "Grab his legs!"

You struggle to pull away, but the two doctors overpower you. Dr Lacey—you can read her name tag—grabs your arms. The man, Stuart, hoists you by your legs.

They carry you through the emergency room, down a hospital hallway, and into a small, dark examining room.

With an evil grin on his face, Stuart locks the door. Then he picks up a tray full of gleaming surgical tools. One of the tools has a jagged, wheel-shaped razor on the end of it. Like a pizza cutter with a super-sharp blade. Another one has pincers!

"Okay," he says. "Let's see what's inside this mummy."

There's no way to escape. Just turn to PAGE 14.

The other guard, the one called George, runs through the marble lobby and lunges at you from behind. His arms encircle you. At the same time, the first guard grabs your legs.

No! you try to scream again. But in the last few moments, your transformation into a mummy has become complete. Your vocal chords have hardened into dry sticks. They won't move.

Suddenly the terrible truth hits you.

To all the world, you are a mummy. Not a kid.

You are a living mummy, a freak of nature, something to be feared . . . and destroyed.

You struggle against the guards, flailing your arms wildly. You kick your dry, brown legs at George's shins. Desperate to escape, you twist your small, leathery body, hoping to slip free.

But you're no match for the guards. They are swift and powerful.

They lift you off the floor, carry you towards the mummy's sarcophagus—and stuff you inside!

Turn to PAGE 33.

"Two thousand dollars?" you say to Web. "You've got to be kidding. This diary must be worth a lot more than that."

Web's smile fades and he gives you an angry stare.

"Okay," he says grumpily. "How about four thousand?"

You shake your head no.

"Eight thousand?" Web suggests.

No.

"This is my last offer," Web says. "Twenty thousand."

Twenty thousand dollars? Is he serious? He's offering you that much money for the mummy's diary? It must be really valuable. Maybe it's worth millions!

You shake your head no.

"Hmmm," Web says, narrowing his eyes. He glares at you as if he hates you. Then his expression changes. The lemonade has arrived.

The Egyptian waiter sets a tall glass down in front of each of you. There's only one problem. His lemonade looks normal but your lemonade is blue!

Turn to PAGE 135.

You need to get these bandages off! And you have to hurry. That guard is going to wake up any second.

Frantically, you claw at the bandages round your neck. Round and round you go. Unwrapping one piece at a time. Some bandages are long, flimsy pieces. Others are short little scraps of cloth. As each one comes loose, you let it drop on the marble floor at your feet.

Finally you reach the last layer of bandages. Slowly, you peel away the thin cloth that covers your skin.

Skin?

No. That's not skin under there. That's ancient, mummified flesh!

It's as hard as football leather. As brown as dried beef. As wrinkled as a sixty-year-old prune!

You whirl round and come face to face with your own image in the mirrored lift doors.

What do you see? Find out on PAGE 77.

116

You decide to throw the croc some sweets.

You are just about to reach into your pocket for some Fruity Bites, when the crocodile suddenly opens his mouth—and attacks you, chomping down hard!

"Aaaahhh!" you scream as you feel his teeth tear through your jeans and begin to pierce your leg.

Crawl over to PAGE 129.

You decide to write a note to your brother and slip it under your family's hotel-room door.

Clumsily, you pick up a pen and clutch it in your gauzy hand. Your hand feels like a paw with all that cloth wrapped round it. So your handwriting looks weird. Messy.

But who cares? Quickly you scribble a note. It says:

"Dear Derek, Help! I can't explain how, but somehow I've been transformed into the mummy. And the mummy has taken over my body! Don't trust that creep. He's just pretending to be me! I'm hiding in the storage cupboard down the hall. Please—come and help me!"

You think a moment. Then you add your birthday and the name of your favourite basketball player. Just so he'll definitely know that it's you.

Then you sign your name.

You sneak out of the cupboard and walk down the hall. Your gauzy feet don't make a sound. You slip the note under the door to the room where your family is staying.

Then you hurry back to the storage cupboard to hide—and wait.

Turn to PAGE 59.

"Whoa, Derek," you murmur softly. "Something really freaky is going on." Trembling, you sit beside Derek on the camp-bed. You read the new entry out loud:

"I have waited forty centuries for this night. The night when the stars are once again just as they were on the night of my birth. The night I can return to life! But now it is not to be. Why? I was too eager. I tried the spell too soon and the diary has fallen from my hands!"

"I knew it!" you whisper to Derek. "I knew I saw his arm move. That's when he dropped the diary."

You go back to reading:

"And now, my diary has been stolen. My life *has been stolen! I must take revenge on the one who steals my magic. Perhaps destroy the thief!"*

Revenge. Destroy! The words are horrible. They jump out at you from the page, a terrifying warning.

Derek lets out a low whistle. "But how did he write that?" he asks. "How did he get in here?"

You remember the words you read earlier. "He—he wrote it with his mind," you explain.

Derek's eyes widen. "But how—"

A knock at the door cuts him off. Who's there?

Turn to PAGE 126.

You stare at the Sphinx, your eyes growing wide.

Is this really happening? Is the Sphinx really talking to you? Or have you finally lost your mind?

Then you spot a crowd of people swarming round the base of the monument.

"Go back!" the Sphinx's voice booms again.

Instantly, the crowd turns. They run from the Sphinx, screaming in terror for their lives!

Fear grips you. You don't know why the people are scared, but suddenly you're scared, too.

So you turn and flee. Sand flies in your face as your feet pound across the desert.

"Cut!" a voice suddenly shouts from a megaphone.

Go to PAGE 122.

Finally a glass door in the spa swings open, and the mummy walks out.

"How . . . do . . . I . . . look?" he asks you in his raspy voice.

"Uh, younger!" you exclaim. "Much younger!"

And it's true. The mummy looks about five hundred years younger. Now he only looks about three thousand five hundred years old.

"Thank . . . you," the mummy says, giving you a small, satisfied smile.

Then he walks out of the health spa and waves goodbye. The last you see of him, his bandages trail behind him as he stiffly strolls down the street.

Weird, you think. But at least it's over.

That's what *you* think.

When you get back to the hotel, you pick up the mummy's diary. And gasp.

There, on the last page—a page that was blank when you left the hotel—you find more new writing. It says:

"Today I met a new friend. A wise friend who knew how to restore my youth. What else does this young person know? I must find out! I will follow this young person for all eternity!"

Oh, well. Here you go again!

THE END

You hang from the mummy's grip, terrified. Your feet dangle several centimetres off the floor. But you still can't wait to hear what the mummy has to say.

"Welcome to the Pyramid Building," the mummy announced.

Huh?

That's it? That's the message from beyond the grave? Rip-off! Bogus!

"Put me down!" you yell and you kick the mummy's knees.

Owwwwww! Your toe bangs into the mummy's bandaged leg, only it's not soft and leathery. It feels hard, more like metal.

Then you hear sounds down the hall. Another figure appears in the dim light of the lobby.

"Over here, Sylvia," the figure calls out. "Found him." The person steps out of the shadows. It's a man in jeans and a sweatshirt, carrying some kind of remote control.

Definitely human.

"What are *you* doing in here?" the man demands.

You can't answer. The mummy still has you by the throat.

Turn to PAGE 136.

Huh? you think. Did someone just yell "Cut"?

You glance over your shoulder and notice another group of people you hadn't seen before.

It's a film crew. An American film crew! It looks as if they're making some kind of adventure picture in Egypt. The crowd of terrorized, running people are all actors and extras. And the voice of the Sphinx is coming from a speaker on the side.

Cool! you think. You wonder who's in the film.

Then you spot him. The star of the film.

Illinois Smith! He's the character in all those action movies about lost treasures and ancient tombs.

Hey—maybe Illinois Smith can help you work out what the mummy's diary means!

What do you think?

Do you ask for his help?

Or do you puzzle it out for yourself?

If you ask Illinois Smith to help, turn to PAGE 54.

If you try to figure it out yourself, turn to PAGE 81.

You decide to take the passageway to the left.

Bravely, you march down the oh-so-dark hall.

You walk a few more steps before you realize that you are alone. Mohammed isn't following you any more.

"Hey, stupid," Mohammed calls. "Why did you go that way?"

"Well," you answer him in your most reasonable tone of voice, "you said to follow my heart. And my heart is on the left. So I thought—"

"I said to follow your *heart*," Mohammed snorts. "Instead, you are thinking too much with your *head*."

Oh. So does he mean you should have gone the other way?

Yes, stupid.

And don't look surprised at being called that name again. You answered to it, didn't you?

Go back to PAGE 15 and take the other passageway, and we won't call you stupid any more.

For a while, you just stare after him into the darkness.

Then you notice Derek on his knees a few paces away from you.

"What happened?" Derek moans. "I feel so dizzy."

"What happened?" you repeat. "I think we've just brought a mummy back to life!"

You help him up. Then you and Derek gaze at each other. Your hands, your arms, your faces. They're all normal again!

No more mummy skin. No more empty eye sockets.

Just two normal kids—on top of Coit Tower.

It takes some quick thinking, but finally the two of you find your way back to the hotel. Without getting caught. Your parents never know that you were gone.

But before you go to sleep, there's one last thing you've got to do. You and Derek hurry over to the Pyramid Building and sneak into the lobby. You just have to find out! Is the mummy still on display?

"Derek!" you cry, as soon as you step inside. "Look!"

The entire lobby is empty. There is no mummy case. No Egyptian display. Everything—every scrap of evidence that the mummy was ever there—has gone.

As if it had never been there . . .

THE END

"He has a computer chip in his brain!" Dr Lacey cries.

Seriously?

You hop off the examining table and hurry over to get a look for yourself. Yup. It's true! There's some kind of weird computer chip in your brain.

For the next three days, the doctors perform six jillion tests on you. Luckily, they don't cut you open.

And guess what? It turns out that the ancient Egyptians were on the verge of discovering computer technologies! At least that's what one of the scientists thinks. The computer chip in your brain is simple, but it works. It allows you to move around.

At first, it's fun being a scientific miracle. You like all the attention. They put your picture in all the newspapers. Reporters come to interview you. They even make a TV special about you.

But after a while, the fun begins to wear off. You start to miss your family. Even Susie, the squirt.

So you decide to write Dr Lacey a note. You want to explain that you're really a kid, not a mummy. And that you want her to help you change back.

But all of your writing comes out looking like ancient Egyptian hieroglyphics! Even you can't read it. It looks like this:

Which, translated, means:

THE END

You clutch Derek's hand. "Don't answer it!" you whisper.

Derek stares at you. "But it might be room service," he protests.

"Room service? Now?" You glance at the clock. It's one a.m.

"Yeah. We ordered food three hours ago, remember?" Derek says. "But it never came. Maybe that's it now."

"Or maybe it's the mummy," you argue.

"Only one way to find out," Derek tells you.

He's right. And as scared as you are, you know you have to find out.

Is there a living mummy on the other side of the door?

"Okay," you grumble. "A quick peek."

"Hold on a second." Derek grabs the diary out of your hands and shoves it under his mattress. Then he nods at you. You cross to the door and take a deep breath.

You open the door just a crack and peer out.

All you can see is a gauzy bandaged arm.

Are you going to open the door all the way?
If no, turn to PAGE 23.
If yes, turn to PAGE 40.

Almost at once, the torch flickers out.

But you don't care. You've made your decision. You're going left, right, right, straight.

In the dark, you walk boldly forward, you arms outstretched at your sides. You run your fingertips along both walls as you go.

Pretty soon, you feel the passageway begin to turn. You've come to your first choice.

You turn left.

You walk a little further and turn right. You keep walking.

Suddenly, in the pitch-darkness, you feel two hands on your face.

"Aargh!" you want to scream.

But no sound comes out. Your voice is choked with fear.

"Boo!" a voice says.

BOO?

Boo who?

Turn to PAGE 134.

128

The Great Pyramid?

You stare at the guard, your head spinning. You've studied Egypt at school. The Great Pyramid is the biggest pyramid in the world. The one that sits in the desert near the Sphinx.

Yup. You're definitely in Egypt.

"But I just came out of there!" you try to explain. "Only it wasn't the *Great* Pyramid. It was the Pyramid *Building*!"

The guard laughs. "Ha! You mean that silly building in America?" He shakes his head and laughs again.

"You've got to believe me," you plead. "And look at this!" You shove the diary towards the guard. "This diary. It was written in English a few minutes ago. And now it's changed to hieroglyphs!"

Before the guard can take the diary, a young man in a tan suit, sun-glasses and a straw hat approaches you.

"I see you have the famous diary of Buthramaman," the man says. He sounds American. "May I see it?"

"Don't give it to him!" the young Egyptian shouts. "Give it to me!"

If you show the diary to the American, turn to PAGE 5.

If you give it to the Egyptian, turn to PAGE 22.

If you turn and run from both of them, turn to PAGE 106.

With all your strength, you wrestle the croc, trying to prise his mouth open. You throw yourself to the ground, whipping the croc off the stairs and over on to his back.

Frantically, you plunge your hand into your pocket. You pull out a few Fruity Bites and throw them into his mouth, next to where your leg is. The croc opens his jaws wide . . . wider . . .

Could it be? Yes! He's letting you escape!

You jump out of his jaws super-fast. But as soon as you're out, the croc smacks his lips together and opens wide.

You can tell from the look on his face that he only wants one thing: more Fruity Bites!

You throw him another handful of Fruity Bites and hurry away.

Uh-oh. Don't look now. With a slap-slap of his stubby legs, the croc follows you! Like a puppy, begging for more sweets.

He snaps his jaws together twice. A warning. And you know what it means. Give him Fruity Bites now—or else!

Well, as long as you can afford to keep buying Fruity Bites, you'll stay alive. BUT YOU'RE IN EGYPT. Where are you going to buy Fruity Bites round here?

Guess you're up the Nile without a paddle. To the crocodile, you look like one big Fruity Bite.

THE END

You still look confused, so Web explains it all to you.

The diary you found on the floor in San Francisco? That was planted there by the FBI. When you went to the basement of the Pyramid Building, you found their fake version of the inside of a real pyramid.

"You *thought* you wandered through the basement and came out in Egypt, but you didn't," Web tells you. "We put a special sleeping gas in the air-conditioning ducts. You fell asleep, and while you were out cold, we had you flown out to Egypt. Your parents knew about this, of course. You woke up in the real pyramid and didn't remember a thing. And the rest has been a test. To see how you handle yourself in tough situations."

"Wow!" you exclaim. "Cool! So now I work for the FBI?"

"Yup," Web says. "You get to skip school for a whole year. And we'll even pay you. Congratulations!" He raises his glass of lemonade in a toast.

"Thanks!" you answer with a huge grin, picking up your own lemonade. Without thinking, you take a big swig.

Oooops. Remember how your lemonade was blue? There was sleeping potion in it! Oh, well. You'll wake up soon, but they'll never let you be a secret agent now. Too bad you made a mistake when you were so close to a happy

END.

Yikes!

You jump, stumbling over Derek's camp-bed. When you catch your balance, you spin round. You see your brother grinning at you in the dim light.

"What are you doing up?" Derek whispers. He lets go of your arm. "Where did you go?"

"Shhhh," you whisper, pointing at Susie. You don't want him to wake her.

Then you tell him all about the mummy. And the mummy's diary.

"Let me see it," Derek demands, sitting on his camp-bed. He loves this kind of thing.

With the light from the bathroom, you can see the diary lying on top of your sleeping-bag. You had to bring your sleeping-bag along, because the hotel couldn't fit another camp-bed in the room.

The diary is right where you left it.

Except . . .

You didn't leave it lying open, did you?

You rush over and pick up the ancient book.

Someone has just written in the diary! And the ink is still wet!

Find out what it says on PAGE 118.

132

You've got to read more of this. It's amazing. The mummy writes it with his mind!

But just then you hear your mother calling your name. "Yoo-hoo." Again she calls you. "Bring Susie and come on!" she says.

You've got to get away so you can look at the diary. You don't want your parents to see it and take it away from you. Not after you've just found it! You scan the lobby for somewhere to go.

You spot a lift.

Hmmm. Maybe you can duck in there and zoom to the top of the pyramid. Finish reading the diary before someone finds you.

Or maybe you should just keep the diary hidden and wait. You don't want to get into trouble with Mum and Dad. And besides, your hotel isn't too far away. You could sneak back here tonight to see if the mummy really escapes. The diary says, "*Tonight* ... I will escape my prison." So what will it be?

If you come back tonight, turn to PAGE 20.
If you take the lift now, turn to PAGE 43.

Somehow you manage to stumble over to the row of bird-faced statues. When you get there, you realize what the nose on the drawing is for.

There among the statues—halfway between the "eyes" and the "mouth"—is a hole in the sand. And some steps that lead down into it.

You hadn't noticed it until now, but the sun is setting against some sand dunes behind you. It looks just like the picture making the nose in the smiley face!

You notice it now because at that precise angle, the sun's rays reach all the way to the bottom of the hole in the sand. And there you see something amazing.

GOLD. Tonnes of it. Coins, little statues, sceptres and crowns. All made of gold. The treasure of King Buthramaman.

So that's why everybody wants the diary. It's a treasure map!

But gold's not all you see down there.

You also see teeth.

Sharp, pointy teeth.

Two rows of them. Grinning up from the gigantic mouth of . . . a crocodile!

As carefully as you can, turn to PAGE 46.

134

The hand taps you again. "You're it!" the voice calls. Then laughs.

You recognize that laugh.

It's your brother, Derek!

You made it! You made it back to the Pyramid Building.

"Derek, what are you doing down here?" you ask.

"Boy, are you going to get it!" he declares. "Mum and Dad are really worried. And they're mad you left Susie all alone. They have people searching the whole building for you. They sent me down here to the basement."

You try to explain to Derek about the mummy, but he only laughs and shakes his head. Then he grabs you by the ear. He drags you through a door you hadn't seen before and up some stairs.

He's right about your parents. They're really steamed up. You can now see why this book is called *Diary of a Mad Mummy*.

You can forget about any more exploring. You're grounded for a month!

THE END

Web glances at your glass of lemonade and smiles. "Special Egyptian recipe," he says. "I thought you might like it. It's sweeter this way." He leans back and waits for you to taste your drink first. He's being awfully polite.

What do you do? You don't want to offend him by not accepting the drink. And you are really thirsty. You can feel sand in the back of your throat.

But the lemonade is blue. And you're not so sure lemonade should be blue.

If you take a sip, turn to PAGE 85.
If you rudely refuse to drink the lemonade instead, turn to PAGE 97.

"Oh, sorry." The man presses a button on the remote and the mummy releases you. You crash to the floor.

A young woman with dark, curly hair rushes into the lobby. You figure she must be Sylvia. She races over to the mummy. "Brad! Is Manny okay?" she asks.

"I think he's fine," Brad tells her.

"What about me?" you grumble. You scramble to your feet. Your neck hurts where the mummy choked you, your toe hurts where you kicked him, and your backside hurts where you landed.

Sylvia turns to you, eyes flashing. "What were you doing to Manny?" She puts her arm round the mummy.

"I wasn't doing anything to him," you protest. "He was trying to kill me!"

Brad and Sylvia laugh. "I think it works," Brad says.

Brad and Sylvia explain that Manny the Mummy is a robot. He's part of a publicity stunt for the exhibit. They were just testing him out to make sure he worked. "We didn't expect anyone else to be around in the middle of the night!" Brad says.

Manny the Mummy is really cool! So are Brad and Sylvia. They let you play with the controls. They even ask you to be part of the promotion! You get to be the one who screams.

THE END

Goosebumps

Reader beware – here's THREE TIMES the scare!

Look out for these bumper GOOSEBUMPS editions. With three spine-tingling stories by R.L. Stine in each book, get ready for three times the thrill … three times the scare … three times the GOOSEBUMPS!

COLLECTION 1
Welcome to Dead House
Say Cheese and Die
Stay Out of the Basement

COLLECTION 2
The Curse of the Mummy's Tomb
Let's Get Invisible!
Night of the Living Dummy

COLLECTION 3
The Girl Who Cried Monster
Welcome to Camp Nightmare
The Ghost Next Door

COLLECTION 4
The Haunted Mask
Piano Lessons Can Be Murder
Be Careful What You Wish For

COLLECTION 5
The Werewolf of Fever Swamp
You Can't Scare Me!
One Day at HorrorLand

COLLECTION 6
Why I'm Afraid of Bees
Deep Trouble
Go Eat Worms

COLLECTION 7
Return of the Mummy
The Scarecrow Walks at Midnight
Attack of the Mutant

COLLECTION 8
My Hairiest Adventure
A Night in Terror Tower
The Cuckoo Clock of Doom

COLLECTION 9
Ghost Beach
Phantom of the Auditorium
It Came From Beneath the Sir

ₕₕₚₚₒ GHOST

**Secrets from the past... Danger in the present...
Hippo Ghost brings you the spookiest of tales...**

Castle of Ghosts
Carol Barton
Abbie's *bound* to see some ghosts at the castle where
her aunt works — isn't she?

The Face on the Wall
Carol Barton
Jeremy knows he must solve the mystery of the face on
the wall — however much it frightens him...

Summer Visitors
Carol Barton
Emma thinks she's in for a really boring summer, until she
meets the Carstairs family on the beach. But there's
something very *strange* about her new friends...

Ghostly Music
Richard Brown
Beth loves her piano lessons. So why have they started to
make her *ill...*?

A Patchwork of Ghosts
Angela Bull
Who is the evil-looking ghost tormenting Lizzie, and why
does he want to hurt her...?

The Ghosts who Waited
Dennis Hamley
Everything's changed since Rosy and her family moved
house. Why has everyone suddenly turned against her...?

The Railway Phantoms
Dennis Hamley
Rachel has visions. She dreams of two children in strange, disintegrating clothes. And it seems as if they are trying to contact her...

The Haunting of Gull Cottage
Tessa Krailing
Unless Kezzie and James can find what really happened in Gull Cottage that terrible night many years ago, the haunting may never stop...

The Hidden Tomb
Jenny Oldfield
Can Kate unlock the mystery of the curse on Middleton Hall, before it destroys the Mason family...?

The House at the End of Ferry Road
Martin Oliver
The house at the end of Ferry Road has just been built. So it can't be haunted, can it...?

Beware! This House is Haunted
This House is Haunted Too!
Lance Salway
Jessica doesn't believe in ghosts. So who *is* writing the strange, spooky messages?

The Children Next Door
Jean Ure
Laura longs to make friends with the children next door. But they're not quite what they seem...

The Girl in the Blue Tunic
Jean Ure
Who is the strange girl Hannah meets at school – and why does she seem so alone?

Reader beware – you choose the scare!

Give Yourself Goosebumps

A scary new series from R.L. Stine – where
you decide what happens!

Choose from over 20 scary endings!